Books by Marion G. Harmon

Wearing the Cape
Villains Inc.
Bite Me: Big Easy Nights
Young Sentinels (2013)

Marion G. Harmon

Bite Me: Big Easy Nights

by

Marion G. Harmon

DEDICATION

"I read that every known superstition in the world is gathered into the horseshoe of the Carpathians, as if it were the centre of some sort of imaginative whirlpool; if so my stay may be very interesting."

Bram Stoker, *Dracula*

ACKNOWLEDGMENTS

I owe a great debt to all the usual suspects, especially family and friends willing to read my first drafts and tell me honestly where I wandered off into the woods. This is a much better story because of you. Also to Ann Rice, Joss Whedon, Stephenie Meyer, and every artist who has ever reimagined and repurposed vampires for their own evil ends.

CHAPTER ONE

Anne Rice sucks. Lord Byron, Bram Stoker, all the rest too. Before they got hold of the horrible legends and turned an unclean spirit possessing a decomposing body into a freaking romantic hero, nobody anywhere thought vampires were nifty.

An unhealthy obsession with bloodsuckers wasn't a problem before the Event. Sure, there were a few delusional psychotics who believed they were nosferatu, and a subset of goth culture that wore fangs with their Victorian lace, but what's the harm? Except for the psychos, I mean. Today it's a whole different story.

Jacky Bouchard, *The Artemis Files.*

This bites.

It had become a mantra, and I repeated it as I watched the fang-action across the room. I'd been haunting Sable's for weeks, and the scene Sable and "Evangeline" were putting on was depressingly familiar. She stood beside his chair (throne, really), all blonde curls and lace over crinoline, while he sipped at her wrist and she shivered deliciously. The rest of his court watched him with greedy eyes. I sipped my Coke and ignored the sad hopefuls watching me.

God. One more night.

The windows open to New Orleans' warm and damp spring night didn't help, and the sweaty crowd around me made me glad I didn't have to breathe. *A deal's a deal*, I reminded myself again. Sable had "requested" my presence in his house three nights a week; in return, he left me alone when I hunted in the French Quarter. Speaking of hunting, it had been long enough between bites that the bodies around me were looking less like people and more like Happy Meals. Time to work.

Looking around for a likely suspect, I caught the eye of a kid with a face full of freckles under bad makeup and a mop of unevenly dyed raven hair. Without lowering my glass, I pointed at the door with my pinky finger and started moving that way myself. He blanched and his Adam's apple bobbed up and down, but he pushed his way out of the crowd and met me in the doorway. Envious stares followed him.

"I don't do public fang," I whispered in his ear, and jerked my head for him to follow me. Down the hall from the crowded parlor was a study where nobody would interrupt us. I took his hand and he flinched a little at my cool grip, but then he squeezed. I almost sighed.

A single red-tasseled table lamp lit the study; Sable liked it dim and probably didn't have a sixty-watt bulb in the house. I sat down on the velvet-upholstered loveseat, straightened my skirts, and patted the cushion beside me.

"I.D.?" I kept my voice low. He looked blank and now I did sigh. "You don't expect me to risk entrapment, do you?"

"Oh, yeah." He nodded eagerly and pulled out his wallet to hand me his driver's license. I held it up. It looked real enough
and declared he was Steve Jansen, eighteen, but I took a picture of it with the camera hidden in my bloodstone cameo broach anyway, then sat demurely while he put it away.

"First time?"

"Na— Yeah." He blushed, and suddenly I didn't have the patience for it. I reached across his lap and took his right hand, pulled it gently towards me, and locked eyes with him.

"It's easy." I put influence into my words and felt him relax under the suggestion. Drawing his hand around my waist made him lean across me. A polite, or at least cautious, boy, he braced against the loveseat so he wasn't lying across my frill-covered chest. The move put his head at an angle, neck in front of me, and despite my influence his Adam's apple bounced again. I added more influence to a gentle "shhh," and watched his pupils dilate till his irises practically disappeared. The pulse in his neck slowed along with his breathing, and when he was ready I leaned forward, opening my mouth.

Just a touch of my teeth and his blood flowed, electric

copper on my tongue. I wrapped my arms around his waist as he went boneless, made a seal with my lips, and started counting. *One Mississippi, two Mississippi, three Mississippi, four...* At thirty I stopped the flow with a lick. He didn't twitch, and I laughed lightly—mood improved as always by the spike of heat in my veins.

"Breathe," I said, and he took a deep convulsive lungful. Pushing him upright, I patted his shoulder. "Hold still." Pulling a handkerchief from my skirt pocket, I wiped away the two little spots of blood left behind before applying it to my own lips. Standing up, I pulled him up with me and over to the door. I waited, holding his hands; there was no way I was letting him out into the crowd in his current state—people could play cruel jokes on someone who'd just been vamped.

When his pupils started to contract I kissed him on the cheek. Putting all the influence I could into it, I whispered "Goodnight Steve, now go home and *don't come back*," and pushed him out the door. He went straight down the hall without looking back, walking fast and without answering any of the calls sent his way. Two shakes and he was past Sable's looming doorman and out the front door. Obviously the suggestion had taken, at least for now.

I shut the parlor door firmly and put my back to it before reaching into my skirt and pulling out my earbug. Wiggling it into my ear, I pushed off and headed for the second, outside door—the other reason I'd chosen the study.

"I am so out of here."

"*Roger that, Night Hunter,*" Paul said. "*I'm parked three blocks south.*" Stepping out into the night, I threw myself into the air, swirling into mist to lift off and climb over the house. I followed the line of wrought-iron streetlamps down Royal Street to where Paul had parked the van just south of St. Louis Cathedral. Floating down and in through the open passenger's window, I pulled myself back together.

Paul started the van. "So Steve is another rescue? Can't do too many of those, you know."

I shrugged. "One less donor-boy won't be missed— and it only really sticks with the first timers. The fang addicts eventually come back."

Looking me over, Paul frowned and fingered the gris-gris pouch he wore under his shirt. I knew what he saw; I'd gone Full Goth tonight to fit in at Sable's. I wore a buttoned-up black skirt, poofed out by an underskirt to give it bounce. Frilled at the bottom, it hugged my rib cage from my waist to just below my breasts, held up by wide shoulder straps buttoned down in the front. My top was a ruffled black blouse with a high neck, closed with my bloodstone cameo—the only splash of color in the whole outfit. Black stockings and button-up boots finished it off. I'd stopped short of putting a bow in my hair and it hung straight and long down my back, but I still looked, maybe, eighteen—younger than I'd been when I died. Certainly too young for the French Quarter after dark, which was why I was here. Talk about entrapment.

Vampires and werewolves and witches, oh my.

Supernatural breakthroughs weren't all that rare, post-Event. In the US most strong breakthroughs responded to their triggering episode by manifesting classic superhero-type powers, but enough people had already been into magic as an alternate lifestyle, or were just purely superstitious, or had a thing for creatures of folklore and fantasy, that we had witches and vampires and werewolves and fairies and demons and other less popular and well-known magical types right alongside the superheroes. And if the capes had made Chicago their home, supernaturals made San Francisco and New Orleans, hometown of Voodoo and vampire-goth culture, their own. It was a mixed blessing for the Big Easy and a job for me.

"Did you confirm Steve's I.D.?" I asked to break the silence.

"Yep," Paul said. "You can spot 'em. Face-recognition picked him out of the Berkley High yearbook. He's not Steve and he's only seventeen. That makes it three for three."

"Good." I smiled and Paul looked away. He didn't like vamps and I didn't blame him. Do mice like cats? The buzz had seeped out of my blood, and I slumped in my seat. In Chicago right now I'd be sitting at a high table in The Fortress, sipping drinks with Hope and watching other capes and their groupies. "Take me home, Paul," I sighed. He nodded and pulled out of his spot.

I certainly didn't need the escort home; I could have misted, or if I was feeling peckish, walked home, maybe collecting a rapist or two on the way. Although that wasn't as easy as it used to be—humans are good at pattern recognition, and the evil-intentioned were acquiring an aversion to young ladies walking alone.

But Grams—Mama Marie—would put such a hex on Paul if he didn't see me to the door, he wouldn't risk it.

We drove back through the Quarter's close one-way streets. Mama Marie lived in one of the narrow two-stories on Esplanade, an old house with its back to the French Quarter and its face to the rest of the world where she could keep an eye on it, lest it make any sudden moves. Not that the rest of the world wasn't useful; when the last hurricane came over the levees and tried to drown New Orleans, capes from all over descended on the Big Easy, got everybody out, and kept the flooding to a minimum.

Didn't matter; up in Chicago we joked about Chicagoland—there was us and then there was the rest of the country. To Grams, the Quarter was the center of the world; the rest was foreign and suspect.

Paul pulled us up half on the curb, and I got out before he could reflexively open my door for me (like me or not, I'm a lady). But he opened the wrought-iron gate and followed me up the short walk that wound through the tiny front yard. Grams kept it covered in planting-boxes and pots full of herbs and climbing plants, with a screen of small yew trees that nearly hid the front porch. He stopped at the porch steps, but stayed while I unlocked the door. Or tried to; sure enough, Grams opened it for me, standing out of my way and nodding to Paul over my shoulder.

I resisted the urge to turn and give him the finger.

Who ever heard of a vampire with a curfew?

Grams closed the door behind me.

"Did you have a good night, Jacqueline?"

"Jacky, Grams. *Jah-kee*."

"Well, child?" What she was really asking was, *did you kill anyone tonight?* There'd only been the once.

I sighed, kissed her cheek. "Yes Grams, I had a good night."

"Best get to your studies, then."

Ten minutes after I'd opened my *Investigation Procedures* textbook on the dining room table, she ambushed me with a brush. One hundred strokes, and she put my hair in a black bow. I didn't say anything. She didn't either. When she disappeared into the kitchen, I closed the book and wandered into the parlor.

I'd never come to New Orleans as a child. Growing up in Southside Chicago, on the other end of the country, I hadn't known about Grams at all until two months ago. Although Grams was dark Creole, with light mahogany skin from the shores of Africa, high French cheekbones, and startling dark blue eyes from God knows where, *Grandpa* Bouchard had been all Cajun—pure French Acadian—and Mom had been, to quote Grams, "whiter than white," which must have made growing up the daughter of a famous voodoo queen tough. She'd rebelled by running as far away as she could inside the US, getting rid of her NOLA accent, and marrying Dad, as down-to-earth a man as had ever been born.

I traced the pictures on the mantle—a cluster of family shots, the most recent of Mom from thirty years ago when she graduated high school. In the pictures, Mom looked just like me: dark eyes and full lips, pale in a way that might have hinted at a romantic ailment in another century. Her midnight-black hair went down to her butt. I only ever remembered her shoulder-length bob, but I also remembered sitting in her lap for one hundred brush strokes until I got too "grown up" to sit still for it.

Did she used to sit still for one hundred brush strokes, too?

Stop obsessing.

Well, if I couldn't study, I could advertise. Anything to put off writing my weekly DSA report—which amounted to *nothing to report*. Nearly eight weeks of nothing to report; two months longer than I should have stayed away from Chicago. Before leaving the parlor, I turned Mr. Robinson right side up. Grams had cut the ward-boss's picture out of the Monday paper and framed it before turning him upside down on a side table—a bit of hoodoo that had to be giving him headaches. Legba didn't object when I took him out of his room and draped him over my shoulders. An albino python, Legba was Grams' animal totem for Papa Legba, her patron loa, and she used him in most of her important rituals. Now I took him upstairs and outside on the balcony.

Esplanade's north and south lanes were divided by a thick strip of grass and trees with a walk down the center. Nowadays the city's old and new money mostly lived in the Garden District or in grand gated communities in the suburbs, but in the old days, when riverboats steamed up and down the Mississippi and New Orleans was one of the busiest ports in the world, Esplanade had been the neighborhood and favored promenade of the rich and elite. With the recent re-gentrification of the neighborhood, all the new Old World lampposts and house lamps showing off the restored homes, the street had become a favorite night-walk again.

I'd left Chicago, left my teammates still rebuilding after the Whittier Base attack, in the middle of a January blizzard. Weather reports said there was still snow on the ground back home. Not here; I stood out on the balcony in the warm spring night, pale as Legba in my goth finery, and passersby got a look at Mama Marie's granddaughter, *le vampir*. A few waved, and I smiled but didn't wave back. Others walked faster. One man stared for awhile before moving on. I actually spotted one of the Big Easy's few capes flying night-patrol overhead. Him I waved to. Then I frowned.

A vampire can see like a cat, and down the street I could see Paul's van, parked in front of a shuttered store. To use Hope's words, *"Hey what?"* I might be Detective Paul Negri's current assignment, but we were both done for the night.

Even before the Event and the appearance of *real*

vampires, vamps had been part of New Orleans supernatural night-scene and in the last couple of years the "vampire's kiss" had become the thrill-drug of choice in the Big Easy. There wasn't much the law could do about it. Make voluntary donations illegal? Most vamps would die since we couldn't just sip blood from cocktail glasses. Require consent forms? When we could bind consent with our influence?

But at least the police could keep us away from minors, on the grounds that in Louisiana you had to be eighteen or older to give blood without parental approval. So since I'd been handy and available, the Department of Superhuman Affairs had sent me south, where I could work with the NOPD and Detective Negri to help keep the dumber and more arrogant vamps off the younger stuff—and quietly keep an eye on things for the feds. Which didn't explain what Paul was doing down the street.

Watching the house? Why? Nobody in their right mind would have messed with Grams, even before I came to stay. Mess with one of New Orleans' reigning voodoo queens? She'd hex them till they *wished* they were dead. No, I didn't believe in voodoo. Really.

Watching me? I was the one vamp the police actually trusted, sort of, even if none of them knew I was Artemis, dark avenger (retired), current superhero (officially), and Scourge of Bad People (Hope's words) back in Chicago.

"Jacqueline?" Gran called from downstairs.

"Coming, Grams." Going inside, I shut the door.

I never considered that Paul might be watching the people watching me.

Chapter Two

Post-Event vampires are an interesting case of a popular stereotype reinforcing itself. The first public post-Event vampire was Barnabas Cross, the British goth-punk singer. The supernatural celebrity locked in the modern vampire template, and although there have been minor variations since, virtually all vampire breakthroughs display the same superhuman powers: superhuman strength, speed, stamina, the ability to mesmerize victims, turn themselves into mist, and unthinkingly perform the minor application of psychic surgery that allows them to drink blood without ripping their donors' throats out. They also tend to share the same traditional and expected vampiric weaknesses: vulnerability to sunlight, holy water, religious symbols, and so forth, although there are some interesting exceptions.

Dr. Mendel, *The Psychology of Supernaturals.*

"Ouch! Dammit!"

The Lone Ranger's theme song went off by my ear and I smashed my head on the lid of my coffin. I fumbled for the light, found my phone.

"Dammit, Paul! It's not sunset!" If it was, my phone would have woken me with Beethoven's Moonlight Sonata, a gift-app from Hope. Who I hadn't called since getting to New Orleans, dammit.

"*Dress normal*," he said. "*We're going to Angels tonight*." Click.

"Shit!" If I'd had room to swing I'd have needed to shop for a new cell phone. Instead I hit the catch, opening the lid, and sat up. Half the reason I wasn't talking to Hope was I didn't want to tell her I was living the lifestyle. I didn't *have* to sleep in a coffin on top of my native earth, but nobody south of Chicago knew that. The dirt under my thin mattress was from Grams' garden.

Hope had first found me in a nice, if small and subterranean, self-furnished apartment with an Asian National Geographic theme. Now I slept in a black coffin—bank-safe steel under wood paneling, but still—in a lamp lit "crypt" behind a secret door in my bedroom. It used to be a walk in closet.

And I slept in black silk. *The secret to a good cover is attention to detail*, my unpleasant but very good DSA minder had said. Repeatedly. In Chicago the only black I'd worn had been my Artemis costume—night-stalking dark avengers were *supposed* to wear black. Mr. Gray had made sure I was outfitted as a goth true-believer.

If I hadn't owed the DSA a favor for figuring out a way to test me—then finding out about Grams and helping me create a new private identity that actually grafted me back onto my family tree—I'd have told them what they could do with their little "side job."

You're going down there anyway. Why not do a little good for the community, collect some background for us, learn about how other vampires live? It'll be easy.

Yeah, right.

At least if it was Angels I could have a little fun.

"Detective Negri is waiting in the parlor," Grams said disapprovingly when I came down the back stairs into the kitchen.

"Really?" My mood lifted, knowing how uncomfortable he had to be.

He always wore his protective gris-gris: dirt from a churchyard sprinkled with holy water, a twist of paper with a verse of scripture on it, other stuff, all in a little cloth bag on a string around his neck. And the way he walked carefully around Grams told me he didn't think it would help a bit if she did her own mojo on him.

Now she aimed her disapproval at me. I'd pulled my hair back in a tail, and I wore smoking-hot black jeans and a tight black athletic top under my black leather jacket, a chain for a belt. The top said *Bite Me* in glittering silver letters. I'd had it made special.

She sniffed, looking like a disdainful duchess.

"And where are you going tonight?" she asked.

"Angels. The club on Camp Street? In the old Confederate Memorial Hall."

"Outside the Quarter?"

"Yes Grams." Then I saw the tea tray.

She smiled with evil innocence. "I thought we should all sit down and be hospitable."

She let Paul escape half an hour later, and I slipped my hand under his arm as we walked out. He'd dressed appropriately too, and in jeans, chains, and leather, with little spikes in his hair and a fake ankh tattoo on his cheek, he looked like a punk Leonardo DiCaprio.

A pale punk DiCaprio; he crossed himself when he knew Grams couldn't see us, and my laugh burbled out. I couldn't help myself.

He gave me a disgusted look. "We're not doing *anything*! Every time she looks at me..." he shivered.

I had preternatural hearing, and I'd heard her talking to Legba once as Paul and I headed out the door early in our arrangement. "Handsome as Satan," she'd said, and "See him *jumpin'*—" before the door closed. No way was I telling Paul any of that.

Angels sat on the other side of the Business District. Surrounded by business buildings and old warehouses, it looked like an old stone church. It got badly burned in a superhero-fight a few years ago, and the cash-strapped city sold it to developers who went bankrupt before they could finish restoring the landmark. A couple of months ago, just before I got here, someone picked it up and converted it; now the nineteenth-century building was one of the hottest nightclubs in town and a favorite hunting spot for vampires after younger prey. The supposedly strict age check at the door meant any vamp could at least claim innocent intent if he got caught with an underage donor on the premises.

They got in, right? So they had to be old enough.

Paul parked his Harley—seized as evidence in a drug-raid, now a sexy prop—right across from the club line. All the tourists coming for Mardi Gras made the lines even longer, but the bouncer recognized us and held the rope aside to let us by. Paul slipped the big guy a fifty to keep an eye on it. Past the pillared arches, we stepped into the vestibule, all shadow and sudden lights to a pulsing techno-beat.

Angels had three dance floors plus an "audience room" and lots of private rooms, and catered more to the vampire-punk posers than the vampire-goths. The difference? Leather and chains, louder music. We hit the main dance floor, melting into the sea of black.

"One enough?" Paul yelled in my ear, scanning the room. I nodded.

The out-of-towners on pilgrimage to the vampire Mecca didn't know me from Eve (or Lilith), but the regulars were happy to point me out and before long I'd attracted a temporary court. Paul reminded them to be respectful so I wouldn't have to, but his focus was gone tonight. He kept looking beyond our circle.

I scanned the crowd but didn't see the Sisters, Belladonna or Acacia. I'd had a hard time not snickering when we'd first been introduced, but at least their vampire names were better than *Sable.* The two Barbie-blonde vamps had appeared on the scene just a week or two after I arrived, but they'd put Angels on the map. If they were out, I might be the only real vamp the club saw tonight; there really weren't that many of us and we mostly kept to our own haunts, and I was fine with that. The exception was the first night of the dark moon, when every vamp in the Big Easy got together and danced the night away at the Midnight Ball in the town's most infamous haunted mansion, Lalaurie House.

It was like *Cats*, only without music by Andrew Lloyd Webber.

I'd only been in town long enough to attend one Midnight Ball—unwillingly and in Sable's company—and I'd been bored out of my mind. All the town's vamps had come to pose for each other, play dominance games, pick out aspiring donors (fang fans paid a steep subscription for the privilege of attending), and settle our little community's political issues under the watchful eyes of the mysterious Master of Ceremonies. The whole thing had been as formal as a Dixie debutante ball, as full of cliques as my old high school cafeteria, and as classy as a stuffed raven.

Like the one in the Lalaurie library. I'd named it Edgar, then renamed it Marc after meeting the dullest fang-boy of the lot.

As if remembering him conjured him up, I spotted Marc Leroy across Angels' dance floor (Le-*Roy*—he was French, which I supposed made New Orleans the only US city fit for him).

I blinked. I never saw Leroy dressed in anything but what I called Boardroom Goth: conservative-cut suit and tie, *everything* in black and nothing shiny. Now he looked as bored as he had at the ball. A good looking blond guy standing next to him said something I couldn't hear above the music, and the two of them bent close in earnest conversation.

What was up with that?

Marc Leroy didn't keep his own court or visit others much, but I'd never caught him hunting and no one knew where he got his own donors. Despite the crush, nobody else invaded Leroy's personal space or even really noticed him, an impressive use of influence. He caught my gaze and raised an eyebrow.

I turned away, felt Paul's hand on my arm.

Paul leaned in and yelled "Drinks," then pushed away into the crowd. I stared after him for a moment, looked back to see that Leroy had also vanished, shrugged and turned to my court. Punk meant less makeup, more hair-gel, making age easier to guess; I had to pick at least one donor or things could get ugly, but I didn't see any clubbers who screamed *minor* yet. Maybe they really were getting more careful at the door?

"Picky, darling?"

I sighed, turning as the space around us widened.

"Acacia, I didn't see you." I bit my tongue as soon as the words were out.

Sister A's eyes narrowed, but Sister B smiled. Belladonna had more of a sense of humor.

"Jacqueline, we've missed you." She linked hands with me and we exchanged air-kisses.

"Sable likes to keep me close," I said, and now Belladonna frowned minutely. *What is with me tonight?*

The Sisters *looked* like sisters, both natural blondes, both cute in the same way, and they dressed to play up the similarities. Tonight both wore more leather and metal than me, upscale biker-chicks. I decided to smooth the waters.

"Seriously Bell, I'm glad I'm here; ruffles and lace make me itch."

"So stay at Angels," she coaxed, dimpling. I sighed theatrically.

"Grams doesn't want me joining anyone's court."

Her smile disappeared and I almost laughed. She brought the smile back, but her eyes were wary. No, they wouldn't mess with Mama Marie.

"Ladies," Paul said, emerging from the crowd with drinks in his hands.

I accepted my Coke and, looking at Acacia, reached up to stroke his neck. He took my fingers and kissed them. Acacia's face darkened, but Bell just rolled her eyes. She didn't mind my asserting my claim, and I relaxed.

Too soon—Bell looked at Paul's unmarked neck and smiled. "Do the two of you need to be alone? Where do you place your lover's bite?"

Paul flushed, and Acacia's eyes widened hungrily. When had she fed last? I smiled and the crowd edged away. Paul didn't move, but he tensed. *Shit.*

Pulling my influence in, I focused on Acacia. "We have plans later," I said.

"Perhaps we could join you?" she whispered. Her hunger beat at me and everyone watching our little scene.

"Some other time." *And Paul's mine, bitch*, I pushed back hard.

Bell gave a high, silvery laugh, and everybody blinked. The club-goers around us relaxed without knowing why.

"You two are so *sweet*." She clasped Acacia's hand and winked at me. "Enjoy the club, and feel free to pick something out. Paul can't be *all* you need."

Paul gave her a bland smile and sipped his Coke.

Chapter Three

Sure I'm dead. I don't eat, sweat, piss, flake, breathe except to talk, or get pimples. No heartbeat (which makes you wonder how my blood gets around, doesn't it?). But in Chicago I know a reservist Sentinel named Iron Jack who can turn into a riveted iron statue with no loss of mobility—and then he doesn't even have blood. *The legal definition of "alive" has become more flexible since the Event, so despite the fact that any coroner would pronounce me DOA if I just held still, I'm legally among the living. There are people who aren't happy with this.*

Jacky Bouchard, *The Artemis Files.*

In the end I grabbed a tourist from New Jersey and used one of the private rooms. The accent was annoying but he didn't talk much, and afterward I danced with Paul till the buzz went away. Then we left. He slipped the bouncer another bill on seeing his bike was still there, and I threw myself on behind him, wrapping my arms around his chest and enjoying the living warmth. He didn't take us far—just around the corner to where General Lee stood atop his pillar in the center of his circular memorial park. Paul crossed the trolley tracks, pulled his bike up on the curb beside one of the power posts, and kicked it up on its stand.

We had the little park to ourselves, and Paul took my hand and led me up the steps and around the base of the pillar. The place was supposed to be lit, but someone kept vandalizing the monument lights and *real* strolling lovers would be insane to hold a makeout-session here. Looking up at the general, I wondered how the upright old soldier would have felt about being memorialized by the Big Easy, the wickedest city in the world.

"Well?" Paul asked.

I shrugged and sat on the marble footing. "Jersey-boy seemed legit, and I didn't spot any babies there tonight. Maybe they really are getting serious at the door."

He nodded, distracted. "That checks. We've been hearing from there less."

He didn't look happy; to Paul a vamp he couldn't catch doing something wrong was just a vamp he hadn't caught.

"So why did we go there tonight?" I asked. "And why—" Then they jumped us.

The rumbling trolley car had masked their run-up, coming around the monument, but they'd been damn quiet anyway—hunters who knew how to stalk prey. One of them clubbed Paul and two grabbed my arms before I had a chance to move, the fourth one swung the stake. It bit and I screamed as my sight went red. Someone waved a cross in my face, shouting Latin at me. Trying to draw breath I didn't need, I spat blood from my punctured lung. Twisting away from the agony, I scrambled backward up the monument steps—the two on my arms clinging like leeches so I pulled us all along, every jerk a fresh burst of agony as the stake in my chest ground against my ribs. The guy who'd swung it lunged after me, tried to fall on it, push it deeper. *What a stupid way to die.*

Then we all heard the howl. A deep-throated roar, it wasn't human.

"Sweet Jesus!" someone screamed, and the guy pushing on the stake disappeared. The two on my arms didn't have time to let go before something pulled them off me and smashed them together. Then I was picked up, screaming again as the stake moved inside me, and found myself dangling from clawed hands as big as dinner plates, staring into animal eyes in a furred and snarling face. Kicking uselessly, I closed my eyes and waited for it to bite my head off. Instead it set me down, pushed me back, and pulled the stake out as I bit down on a shriek.

Putting my hand to my side, I breathed in and felt blood bubble from the punctured lung. Damn it, Jersey Guy was going to waste. But the terror of the attack, of the huge *thing* in front of me, faded as it failed to eat me. My attackers stirred and groaned; a blood-freezing growl and they lay still, trying to not even breathe. *I* didn't want to move, but where was Paul?

Sirens. Paul must have pushed the panic-button. If he wasn't too badly hurt—

I saw the cloth bag hanging from the thing's neck, and started to laugh. Which hurt so bad I was laughing and crying when the cops flooded the park.

***

"Seriously, Paul. What the hell?"

The police arrested everyone in sight, although ambulances had to take two of them to the hospital first. They took Paul and me in as well, just for appearances. The paramedics looked like they wanted to do something for me but couldn't think of what, making me laugh again; the blood had stopped flowing by the time they'd arrived.

Somebody gave Paul a crime-scene coat to go over the knee length spandex shorts that were apparently wolf-man wear—at least they were the only piece of clothing that survived his transformation (and I wondered how it felt when he burst out of his boots)—but we still got stares as we walked into the French Quarter Precinct. They put us in one of the interrogation rooms, and I wondered why they kept it so chilly until I realized it was me. Blood loss. Dammit. *Think about anything else.*

"So?" I pushed.

Paul watched me carefully. Blood loss didn't weaken vampires right away—it made us hungry first.

"Later," he said.

"Later? You just...and—later? Seriously?"

He shook his head, looking at the one-way glass. "Are you going to be alright?"

"They keep us here long and I'll go nuts for the first paper-cut I see, but if we get out soon I can pick up something on the way home." I looked down at myself, groaned. My shirt and jeans were soaked in Jersey Guy's blood, the jacket not much better off, no way I could hide what had happened.

Paul looked at the window again, then pulled back his sleeve and held out his wrist.

"What—"

"Shut up. Just don't try and vamp me. It may be awhile and we can't have you going crazy in here. Besides, Mama Marie will kill me anyway, letting you get hurt."

"But you hate—"

"My foul, my penalty. Dammit, don't argue."

Argue? I'd focused like a laser on the suicide-vein. With a sigh, he held it up so I barely had to lean forward. I gripped the arms of my chair—if I grabbed him now I'd leave bruises—my lips kissed his skin, and with a touch of my teeth his living blood flooded my mouth. He flinched, but didn't break the seal.

One Mississippi, two Mississippi, three Mississippi, four... I'd been told the bite feels like breath on sensitized skin, running through all your veins. It's practically hallucinatory when amplified by influence, but even doing it straight like this Paul had to be feeling it hard. I forced myself to stop at thirty, and raised my head. His jaw was locked, but he hadn't looked away or closed his eyes.

"Done?"

I nodded.

"Good." He pulled the sleeve down over the tiny marks. *We won't speak of this again,* his eyes said.

Fine. I sat back, looking at the ceiling while the buzz wore off. I still had Grams to worry about. She'd been dead-set against my participation in Operation Younger Stuff from the beginning; the only reason she'd gone along with it was it was the price for the Department of Superhuman Affair's legalizing my Bouchard name and creating the semi-fictional background that went with it so nobody knew I was also the Jacky Siggler that died five years ago in Chicago. Besides—

Wait.

"What do you mean, your foul your penalty?"

Paul shrugged. "I knew someone was watching you. Figured I'd lure them into the open with an easy opportunity—I just hadn't realized how many."

"You used me as *bait*?" The buzz was definitely gone.

Chapter Four

Superheroes do good and fight supervillains. Vampires pose a lot and fight each other, mostly with dramatic but harmless little dominance games since we're as self-centeredly amoral as cats. But once in a while we have to fight hunters, idiots who believe that we're Evil with a capital E. Can you blame them? If it looks like a duck and quacks like a duck, right?

Jacky Bouchard, *The Artemis Files.*

Lieutenant Emerson's entrance kept me from hurting the rat-snake bastard.

"Evening Jacky," he said, closing the door and dropping a stack of files on the metal table. "You've created quite a night for everybody."

I slouched, folding my arms. "Negri here set the stage."

"I know—he had two extra units on standby all night.

Nobody's blaming you, child. Did you recognize any of the men?"

Emerson (*Ralph W.* Emerson, and he didn't think it was funny) was a dark, dark Creole, bald and cadaverously thin; he always wore black suits and all he needed was a top hat to play Baron Samedi. A senior detective who kept passing up advancement to an administrative job, he worried me enough for me to let the *child* comment pass.

I shook my head and Paul put his elbows on the table, pre-empting the debriefing. "I spotted them five nights ago," he said. "But only the two. Couple of the clubs, always nearby but not close. Last night I saw one of them watching Mama Marie's. Figured them for hunters, me."

"And you thought you'd flush them out yourselves, no close support? Detective, I know you haven't been here long but we don't work that way."

Paul flushed, ducked his head and nodded. "Won't happen again. What did you find out?"

"That you were damn lucky." Emerson snorted, sliding the files across the table. "These bayou boys had a goal and a plan." He nodded at me. "They were hunting you, not just any vamp. Their ringleader, Robert Dupree, blames you for turning his sister—he and his cousins figured they'd test the old stories that the way to end a vampire curse is to kill the vampire that gave it."

"*Me?*"

"You. Doesn't matter that anyone who knows anything about breakthroughs knows that a vampire can't create another vamp, any more than any other breakthrough can duplicate his condition. That bit's still myth, thank God, but his sister was a wannabe-vamp, came to town looking to join someone's court. Last he heard from her was a text to her cousin going on about meeting you somewhere—described you down to your *Bite Me* shirt and leather jacket. Said she was working up the nerve to offer herself to you."

"So on that he thinks I *turned* her?"

"That, and she's Acacia now, one of the Sisters. He claims that when he found her at Angels she didn't even recognize him."

"*Damnation*," Paul said. "What are the odds?"

Emerson didn't look away. "That she got a vamp to kill her hoping to be turned? Not bad. And really got turned? Not good."

It was the ugliest of the vampire con games; convince some poor sap you'd turn him for enough money, let him taste your blood a couple of times in the setup, take the cash, drain him dry somewhere private, dispose of the body. Breakthroughs, supernatural or superhero, were one in thousands—not much chance of delivering on your promise. I hadn't caught wind of any of those sickoes, but Emerson had seen a few before I came to town.

And I knew something Emerson didn't. *What if it's not a con this time?*

I'd have been corpse-pale if I wasn't already.

Paul leaned in. "You can't be blaming Jacky—"

"No," Emerson said, but he watched me like cop watched a perp. "So why are we still here?" I asked. I had to get out.

"Your cover. If you weren't working for us you'd be our main suspect. So now that we've had this 'interrogation,' we're going to cut you loose."

"And them? What happens to them?"

"There's not a jury that would convict, but we'll press charges anyway. They're both a danger and a flight risk, so we can keep them till the hearing if we need to—even till the trial. While we do our own investigation."

He locked eyes with me. "Because whoever accidentally turned her instead of killing her will run the game again. Probably ran it before. So we find him."

I nodded. Gathering up the files, he stood as I ground my teeth and tried not to look at my "partner."

Well, hell. Paul thought vamps were squirrelly enough already; he was going to *hate* this. I took a breath. "Emerson? There's something you should check out."

He stopped shuffling papers. "Yes?"

"When did you serve your last blood warrant on Acacia and Belladonna?"

"Two weeks ago. Why?"

Even for a heavy-drinking vampire, recoverable blood-trace from their donors lasted two or three weeks in their veins—which was what made our job possible. I and other observers ID'd underage donors, the precinct got warrants for their DNA and matched them against samples taken from vamps with blood warrants. Penalties started at heavy fines and escalated to jail time.

"Because," I said quietly, "if she's really another

vampire's progeny—even if he didn't intend to make her—they might have a blood relationship."

"A *what*?"

Great. How to explain the Bats and the Bees?

I spread my hands. "The whole turning thing, even the scam, requires blood-swapping, right? And it's hardly universal, but some vamps have this whole dominance and territorial thing going. If you want to share a more aggressive vamp's "territory" you have to accept his dominance—usually by sharing his blood."

Emerson's eyes sharpened. "Not by accepting his bite?"

"You'd think, but no."

Paul shifted beside me. "Have you..." he trailed off, obviously thinking of my arrangement with Sable. I smiled, showing fang.

"He knows better than to try it, but his whole court thinks I drink from his vein. Anyway, Sable's really *really* into 'Lucys'—blonde ingénues—not Minas like me." I flipped my now very mussed black mane.

Emerson grunted. "So you're saying Acacia might owe her 'sire'...what?"

"Blood fealty. At the very least, I'd think they'd swap blood once in a while so he could reassert his dominance."

The lieutenant looked deeply disturbed, and it surprised me that he didn't know this little twist of vampire politics; understanding supernaturals was what he *did*.

"So how does a blood warrant help us?" he asked.

"Wouldn't we just find traces of whomever he'd recently bit too?"

I shook my head. "That itself might be worth something. Like Black—like my teacher says, 'no intelligence is wasted.' But it doesn't matter how long we've been dead, all of us still carry a little of our own blood. So if you research every old blood warrant…"

Now he nodded. "We might be able to isolate vampire-markers, and if there are two sets then one of them probably belongs to whomever turned her. That's *good*, Jacky. I'll have forensics get right on it, thank you. Anything else?"

"Nope. I'm out of here." I stood and finally glanced at Paul. He looked… like Paul, no evidence of how he'd taken it.

"Drive safe now," Emerson said. "And Jacky? Give my regards to your grandma." He smiled, like he knew she was going to come down on his head like the wrath of God for letting me get hurt in one of his operations. And looked forward to it.

Mama Marie vs. Baron Samedi. That was a throw-down I'd have paid big money to see any other time; now I didn't want them coming near each other.

Paul kept a change of clothes in his precinct locker, and I kept my mouth shut while he dressed and we slipped out the back. Once out the door I stepped into mist. He called my name, but I was gone like yesterday. I floated up into the night, arrowing for home. The trip was a stretch but I didn't rest once, not till I'd misted in through the vent down to my safe bedroom. Pulling myself together, I stripped and rolled up the sticky remains of my outfit, threw them under the bed. Then I went right into the shower, turning it up to scalding.

I felt colder than the grave, but corpses don't shiver. *What are the odds?*

One night after a successful outing, possibly the one that had made Angels more careful, Paul asked me why *I* hated vampires; after all, I'd had to have been obsessed with them to become one, right? Breakthroughs, didn't we all make ourselves what we were?

Not true, but I couldn't tell him why.

There were no vampire "families" since normally each vampire was a lone breakthrough, a one-off just like any other superhuman, but there was no end to the stories of secret Master Vampires capable of intentionally turning their victims, creating vampire *progeny*—the reason why the con was so easy to pull. I'd hoped there'd really only ever been *one*. The one who'd slaughtered my parents and turned me. The one I'd staked, decapitated, burned to ash, scattered on Lake Michigan.

But now I might not be the only vampire progeny.

I tried to feel the water beating my icy skin.

You are mine, he'd said. And proved it by killing everyone else I'd belonged to.

Grams heard me and came upstairs, but not before I'd broken every bit of glass in the bathroom and Paul's blood swirled in the drain.

Chapter Five

On October 15th at 10:13 pm, 9-1-1 recorded a hysterical call from Jacqueline Siggler, screaming, and what sounded like an animal attack in the home of Tony and Charlene Siggler. Responders arrived less than five minutes later to find the adult Sigglers dead, mauled by an unidentified animal, and their daughter missing. A protracted neighborhood search found neither the animal nor the missing daughter, and the mystery remains unsolved.

David Roush, *Strange Crimes.*

How can someone as old as Grams be so strong? She pulled me out of the water and glass and wrapped me up, nearly carried me downstairs to the kitchen. Eventually the smell of coffee pulled me out of my funk, and I lifted my head off the table to find a cup in front of me. Ethiopian shade-bean: she'd raided my stash. A little serving pitcher of English cream joined it while the teapot whistled. Grams considered coffee a foreign perversion.

I wrestled with the robe she'd wrapped me in, finally got the arms right, and flavored my cup while she steeped her tea. She only left the kitchen long enough to let Paul in; I vaguely remembered hearing her call him after getting me to the kitchen table.

"Holy shit, Jacky," Paul said, looking me over. With all the tiny cuts lacing my skin, I must have looked like I'd been wrestling rabid kittens. "Are you—"

"Fine," I said. "I'm fine."

Grams snorted and pointed to a chair, dropping a cup of coffee in front of it. He looked at it like it was a bomb, but sat gingerly as I added a little more cream to my cup.

"Are you really—"

"Detective Negri," Grams said, voice cold. "You will tell me why my granddaughter snuck into the house tonight and decided to redecorate her bathroom in red."

"Grams!" My teaspoon rang on the table. "Paul didn't have anything to do with that!"

"Oh? You were not with him, tonight?"

"I—yes, I was. But it's just... news. Someone's... Dammit, Paul!" I turned on him. "Why didn't you tell me you were *furry*?"

"Fu—" That stopped Grams, whatever she'd been expecting to hear.

"We got attacked by hunters tonight, Grams. Paul went all wolfman on them, saved my ass."

"Language, Jacqueline."

I rolled my eyes. "Saved my *butt*." Who knew the

voodoo queen of New Orleans would have so much in common with the Grande Dame of Chicago? Mrs. Lori would love her.

"Saved my *life*," she corrected with a smile, which iced over when she turned back to Paul. "And who attacked my granddaughter?"

"Grams, focus. The police have got them and aren't letting them go. Paul. Furry."

She nodded, eyes sharp. "Lycanthrope, but not *loup-garou*, yes?"

I blinked. "Loop-what?"

"Nope," Paul said. "No curse, ma'am. My momma's family is rural Italian." He sighed. "Different stories, so I'm *Benandanti*—a Good Walker." He took a sip, looked down.

"That's good coffee, *chèr*."

"Thank Grams—*I* wouldn't have made it for you."

"Jacqueline!"

I sighed and Paul had the nerve to actually give me a wink. "*Non*, Madam Bouchard," he said. "I deserve it, me." His Cajun English was getting thick.

I sat back. He was making it hard to stay mad. "So your mom's family tradition shaped your breakthrough."

He nodded, grimacing.

"But the Negri family, all bayou Cajun, we. Back home the *loup-garou* a bogyman, hunts horny teenagers out after curfew you know?"

Grams nodded, understanding. No, Church Pointe, Acadia would be no place for a wolfman; they'd always be waiting for him to eat somebody.

After that the conversation wandered where I hadn't wanted it to go, back to the fun we'd had earlier. Grams told Paul to let Emerson know she *expected to see him*—a comment that went right past me at the time. Miracle of miracles, now that her direst expectations had been fulfilled, she was actually warming to Paul. A little.

I hadn't left so much blood in the bathroom that I needed another drink tonight (usually I was good for two or three days) but I actually found myself yawning and trying not to show fang. Grams, who insisted on treating me like the teenager I wasn't anymore, not even on paper, shooed me up to bed after making Paul promise to stay. After using her bathroom to clean up, I crawled into my coffin and locked it, sealing out the world. I slept like the dead.

My eyes snapped open as I rose out of my dreamless, breathless sleep, and I lay listening for a moment before opening my coffin.

Letting myself out of my crypt and into my room, I stripped out of my nightgown (I preferred to sleep in a tank top and sleep-shorts, but no, I had to be *authentic*), and threw on black jeans and a black midriff-baring cotton cami with little white bats on it (*authentic*, but still better). Snapping my moonlighting gear to my belt under my jacket and thumping down the back stairs into the kitchen, I could hear Grams with a client. Low chants and the smell of scented candles leaked under the parlor door.

Pulling out my stash and pouring beans into the hopper of my hand-mill coffee grinder, I milled a measure fine and sighed as the rich smell of ground bean rose to overpower the candles and fresh herbs. Unpacking my coffee-box, I carefully scraped the pile of grounds into the terracotta bowl, poured the filtered rainwater Grams had left steaming over it, stirred with my wooden spoon, and counted. At sixty seconds, I poured the brew through my gold-wire coffee strainer, topping off my matching mug. Rinsing my tools, I grabbed the cream pot and sat down.

Blood gave a kick, but any vamp who claimed it was ambrosia was a pretentious ass and when I wasn't thirsty I preferred anything that didn't taste of hemoglobin. I paid homage to the Bean of Life and watched the parlor door.

Grams hadn't led big voodoo ceremonies in years (she said she wasn't athletic enough anymore, and I tried not to imagine what she meant), but she still consulted and I wondered what tonight's client wanted; gris-gris to snare a lover's interest? Luck-mojo? Or maybe a curse, although Grams swore she only ever hexed with karma-curses—evil rebounding on the evil-doer.

I didn't rush, but neither did they. A careful peek out the heavily-curtained kitchen windows told me the sun had completely set, and I washed my mug and set it in the drainer. I wasn't on the job tonight—a good thing since I wanted to find my own answers, the big one being if I needed to kill somebody. And I had to start in the last place I wanted to look.

I needed more information, and I'd been avoiding even *thinking* about what that meant.

Going back upstairs, I fired up my laptop—an older

model, but overpowered for what I needed it for. Before I'd left Chicago, Blackstone had turned it into an unhackable fortress of encrypted files; he'd even installed a "hard-burn safety" so any unauthorized attempt to physically recover anything would result in an expensive and useless melted lump. Five security answers later, plus three hand signs witnessed by my webcam (the 'peace' sign, the middle finger, and the 'okay' thumb and forefinger) I was in, staring at a file folder I'd sworn I would never open.

Chapter Six

An Omega Event is a breakthrough-created superhuman capable of ending civilization as we know it. The Department of Superhuman Affairs shut down two that I know about: a human-to-computer intelligence transformation that almost took over every internet-linked computer system in the world, and a breakthrough who sucked anyone who got too close to him into a group-mind that spread like a psychic virus. On that one the DSA "quarantined" an entire town, and drone cameras recorded its disappearance microseconds before the nuclear missile "sterilized" it. The public didn't know about those; the DSA blamed the first on a hacker's conspiracy and the second on a wormhole that sucked the town into an alternate world (hey, it might be true). They only told me about them because they needed my help to determine whether or not I was the starting-vector for the third.

Jacky Bouchard, *The Artemis*

Files.

By freeing me from my sire, the Teatime Anarchist had short-stopped the potential Vampire Plague future, but the future-files he'd posthumously left to Shelly and Hope were all about the futures that would never happen now, at least not the same way. Before I left Chicago—less than two weeks after the Whittier Base attack—Hope had given me TA's "Vampire File", a copy of all the collected future data from the plague that never happened.

I *really* wasn't interested in my Might Have Been as Vlad the Raving Psycho's enthralled pet, so I'd left it alone while I'd been the DSA's guest at Camp Necessity and even coming to New Orleans hadn't convinced me to open it. After all, the vamps down here were *nothing* like psycho-Vlad. At least I'd thought that, anyway. Blackstone would be disappointed in me; years learning street smarts as a night-stalking black-clad vigilante, months learning the paranoid art of threat analysis from him, and I'd turned my back on my most valuable data source.

I opened the file and started reading.

If my stomach acted at all like a living one, I'd have been sick.

It looked like TA hadn't been completely honest with me—not that the twisty, sneaky time traveler who'd saved my soul from Vlad had ever told anybody the whole story about anything.

TA had told me that Vlad would have started a vampire plague that burned down Chicago if I hadn't staked him—but the file of future news reports and analysis followed the outbreak from Chicago to LA, Washington, New York, and Boston. Statistically it was impossible that *one* master vampire could have done all that; the theory had been that maybe one vampire in thirty had proved capable of creating progeny herself. To make it worse, progeny like me that weren't into all things vampire to start with didn't inherit a lot of the traditional phobias and compulsions.

Like allergic reactions to religious symbols, or needing an invitation to enter a home. With lots of supervamps like me, not even the superheroes could stop the body count from becoming an unreal statistic—worse than the Big One, last year's mother-of-all-quakes. Instead iron curfews, fortified sanctuaries, cadaver-dogs, quarantines, cremation of the dead, and nationwide martial law had finally ended the Killing Nights. I watched a helmet-cam video of an armored special forces team burning a screaming nest with flamethrowers, and wondered when I'd died—and how many victims I'd drained first.

One Master Vampire in thirty. I closed my eyes.

Thanks to TA, I'd been psycho-Vlad's only progeny; with him dead and ashes the Vampire Plague had become just one more Might Have Been. But New Orleans was Vampire Central and there were around twenty of us here now. How many more scattered around the world? When I'd approached the DSA and told them I was progeny, a *made* vampire, they'd nearly dropped a brick. They'd yanked me out of Chicago with barely time to pack, and I'd spent three weeks at their Camp Necessity while they made sure I couldn't sire progeny myself (my whole reason for telling them). They'd been right to worry; all it would take was one.

Was a new master vamp in town? The DSA really needed to know this—looking out for stuff like this was really what they'd sent me here for. But I didn't *know*. If I raised the alarm all hell would rain down on New Orleans' vamps, and if I was *wrong*...

I closed the laptop and sat in the dark for long minutes before heading out.

I needed to learn a lot more about Acacia's story and about Angels, which meant talking to a vamp who'd been in town longer than I had—preferably one as unconnected with the circle of courts and establishments as I was, who "floated" around town as much as I did. Much as the man made me want to hurt him, my best possible source was the only other vampire I knew who didn't keep a court or belong to one: Marc Leroy.

I checked my moonlighting gear: mini-epad, ID to prove that I really was old enough to drink, if only just (it was fake; *nobody* would believe a driver's license that said I was twenty-five), my holdout pistol (the little Kel-Tec 9mm I hadn't had the other night), and plenty of folded cash. I added a blood-kit; we'd never caught Leroy in our net, but a voluntary check would rule him out as Acacia's sire, whatever he'd been doing at Angels.

So naturally I couldn't find him. He wasn't at his fencing school, the *Salle D'Armes*. One of the teachers told me he'd accepted a bodyguarding job for a Hollywood celebrity come to town. Since he might not get back much before dawn, I didn't wait.

Vamps had to support themselves somehow. Sable lived off of "gifts" from his court and a door-fee at his place. Angels paid Acacia and Belladonna to hold court there, like having a popular house band. I was studying for a private investigator's license—the clichéd occupation of "good" vampires—as part of my cover story. Marc Leroy taught fencing and worked as a high-end bodyguard.

As expensive as Leroy was (I'd heard you could buy a car with what he got paid for a night, which had me considering a side-career) only people who wanted to be *seen* with him hired him so I could probably find him where the party was. The party was everywhere this close to Mardi Gras, but checking a couple of buzz sites on my epad gave me a target; Chris Block was in town and the famously hard-partying singer had been spotted crawling up Bourbon Street, going club to club with an entourage.

This year Mardi Gras was late and spring was early, and I heard the brass notes of practicing bands as I floated over the Quarter in the warm night. When people think Mardi Gras they tend to picture the booze-chugging, boob-flashing, bead-throwing party that takes over Bourbon Street, but it's a city-wide celebration and the big parades don't even enter the Quarter's narrow streets anymore. And Mardi Gras is only the last day of Carnival, the day with the most parties and parades; the party started on Twelfth Night in January and danced through the city till the stroke of midnight sternly announced Ash Wednesday and the beginning of Lent.

Dropping down to street level, I drifted invisibly through knots of tourists thronging Bourbon Street's bars and clubs. The tickling tones of *If Ever I Cease to Love* drifted out of a piano bar, mixed with laughter and drunken karaoke to some new hip-hop hit. I didn't feel any other vampires in the wind, but Bourbon Street wasn't really one of our favorite haunts; the party here wasn't about *us*.

It took me over two hours to find him; contrary to TV scriptwriters, we didn't come with vampire-detection radars and the only time I could *feel* another vampire was if they were using influence or if they were dispersed into mist and close enough for me to feel their drifting essence. I finally ran him down in *Fais-Do-Do*. Bodies packed the Cajun club so tight that if Chris hadn't been on a table screaming along with a band covering his songs, his biggest fans couldn't have spotted him from ten feet away. The band was covering badly, but he didn't care.

Leroy obviously didn't care either; the noise had nothing to do with him. Propping up the wall beside Chris' table, he looked bored but his eyes tracked me as I pushed through the crowd. A little influence let me nudge heavier drunks aside without being obvious until I joined him by the wall.

"Where is the licorice cupcake?" he asked when I squeezed in beside him.

"Bite me." When Sable had brought me to the

Midnight Ball, I'd worn the frill-and-lace perkigoth confection I wore for his court. Le-*roy*'s droll dismissal of my outfit—which I didn't like either—hadn't endeared him to me.

It hadn't helped that *his* severe black outfit had been tailored tightly enough that if he'd raised his arms over his head his armpits would probably have come unseamed. With his whip-thin, hard-muscled physique, he didn't need any decorations to look yummy.

Yummy and bored and dismissive, like tonight.

"Charming," he said.

"Bite me."

He sighed. "Since you are here, Sable requires something. And please don't repeat yourself."

I almost said *bite me* again just to poke him.

"I'm not Sable's," I said instead. Chris hit a warbling high note and I winced. "When is your job done?"

He raised an eyebrow, tapping his thick gentlemen's cane against the hardwood floor. With most guys canes are a costume prop, an affectation, but I was willing to bet that for him it was a weapon.

"I would guess no more than an hour, given my employer's current rate of consumption. In any case this is his last stop before taking the party back to his rooms. Join us til then?"

"Sure, torture me."

"You are not being paid to stay."

I ground my teeth. When he got so patronizingly *French* I wanted to shoot him, but I settled in. We had to make an interesting picture together—me in black jeans and leather jacket, him dressed for a state dinner. The pencil-thin beard he wore only made him look more cultured and sophisticated, and our very different complexions—me pale as the moon, him the shade of coffee with cream—completed the contrast.

A little more influence got the server to believe that I was twenty-one (half the time nobody would accept my ID otherwise). She delivered my order of a glass of Blue Moon, a Belgian *witbier* I'd learned to like, and I settled in.

We didn't talk much, and nobody paid attention to us. I did ask where he was from; his diction was perfect but his accent bugged me. He didn't sound Cajun, and it turned out he really *was* from France, from Orleans, ironically enough. He wore a heavy silver ring with a *fleur-de-lis* on it, like someone else might wear a college ring.

Chris had an amazing tolerance for alcohol, but his minders got him moving when it looked like he'd have to be carried if he had one more. The party animal image was good, falling-down drunk, bad, and presumably he had his choice of liquor and drugs waiting back in his hotel suite anyway. Apparently he'd rented the Hotel Monteleone's penthouse suites so he could hang in the Quarter till the end of Carnival.

I got to watch Leroy work. He never looked at Chris, eyes moving over the press of partiers and street crawlers around him as we walked. The tight one way streets of the Quarter, packed as they were in the run-up to the big night, left no room for a caravan large enough for Chris' entourage; instead we walked to the hotel, Leroy on alert the whole way. He asked me to wait in the lobby while he got everyone upstairs; after that they were a problem for hotel security.

"My place?" he inquired when he returned.

It didn't sound like a friendly invitation, but I agreed and we set off. It felt strange, rising into mist with a keen awareness that he floated upward ahead of me. I couldn't *see* him—I felt him where our boundaries touched and mingled, and it distracted me so much that I didn't notice the other vamps. They dropped out of the night air, and suddenly I was flesh and blood in the grip of gravity. I hit the roof below hard enough to knock the wind out of me if I'd needed to breathe. Leroy yelled, which meant he'd gone corporeal too, but my attention was taken by the hooded and masked vamp swinging a machete at my neck.

What the hell?

Life-and-death fights aren't conducive to analytical thought and I hadn't survived by asking *why* questions in the heat of the moment; I rolled away from my hooded attacker to come to my knees with Kel-Tec in hand, put three shots through his center of mass *pop pop pop*. He staggered as they punched him, kept coming, and I fell back into mist as his swing cut air where I'd been. He leaped into mist after me, and *again* I hit the roof, staggering, pulled back into flesh.

I skipped the *how did he do that?* and went with the instinct that told me where he'd pull himself together. His re-fleshed knee met my boot—a lucky kick. He yelled, fell, lost the machete, and I put the fourth bullet through his forehead. Then I dropped and rolled away as *another* vamp went solid above me. He landed wrong and I shot him too. Behind me I heard the ringing hits of swinging blades, turned, caught a flash of Leroy facing off a pair with a sword of his own—*a sword cane?*—before spinning back to my own fight. My first attacker shook off the headshot, snatched up his blade, and whirled into mist as I backed toward Leroy and tried not to trip on the uneven roofing. His buddy kept his own machete pointed at me.

I felt Leroy dance through the mist and back at least twice—not sure how I knew it was him—and then his back found mine.

"Friends?" he asked without turning.

"Not mine."

"Know them?"

"Seriously? Under the hoods?"

He laughed. "Then fly!" he barked.

I reflexively leapt into mist, felt him do the same and pass *through* me, fell back into flesh ahead of the will that pulled at me (why had nobody told me a vamp could *do* that?), landed on my first attacker and used my fistful of gun to club him hard. He staggered but pushed me away, then collapsed to the roof as his head flew off. Leroy flicked blood off his sword as I dropped my useless gun to grab his victim's machete, and we turned back to back as the three left took flesh around us.

They spaced out to ring us in, machetes swinging, three vamps in Mardi Gras masks under black hoodies, watching as we spun slowly. No threats, no posing or demands, just careful steps in a weird parody of a circle dance.

I was fine with not talking.

The two in my line of sight misted and I felt Leroy do the same before I followed myself. Angling on the one to my right, I *felt* him changing and raced him back into flesh. He got there first, but misjudged; I came down behind him, swung with a scream, and his head leaped away in a fan of blood.

"Yes!" I shrieked, spinning around. Two of the bastards down, two to—

I heard Leroy shout, felt the bounce as I hit the roof, but couldn't feel anything else. Or move except to blink at the pair of boots I was staring at. *What the hell...*

Chapter Seven

"Near-death experiences? I'd give my Taylor Swift collection to have only near-death experiences."

Recorded interview from The Artemis Files.

"Aah!" I bolted upright, choked on blood, spit, tried again.

"Take it easy," somebody soothed.

"What. I. Aaaaa, *shit!*" Words could not express the awful realization, just before thought disappeared entirely, that I'd been decapitated. I wrapped my hands around my neck and they came away sticky. The ghost of pain, like a necklace of fading papercuts, told me where the slice had been.

If I'd been alive I'd have been hyperventilating—instead I spit more blood as I tried to understand where I was. I'd been laid out on somebody's kitchen counter under a hanging forest of steel pans and cutlery. In a kitchen that either belonged to a vampire or someone with an obsessive-compulsive cleaning disorder.

"Easy," Leroy said again as *thirst* hit me hard enough to freeze coherent thought. I got as far as *I need* before his arm was in front of my face and I found myself sloppy-sucking on his wrist. I didn't think to count, but he did and pulled away after a minute. I still felt like I could drink the sea, but at least I could think.

I looked down at myself. My jacket and cami stuck to my skin, tacky with blood. Leroy came around beside me as I pulled at the ruined top.

"What hap— What happened?" I choked again, voice thin. Had my headless body reflexively tried to breathe, pulled blood down into my lungs?

Leroy's suit jacket was gone, his sleeves rolled up, but none of my blood was on *him*. He looked curious, like he'd gotten home and wandered into the kitchen for a late snack to find me lying on his preparation counter.

"The other two left when one lost a hand," he said. "I brought you here."

"They *chopped my head off!*" I shrieked, using up my lungful of air. I took a breath, dialed it down, asked the all-important question. "How am I alive?"

He actually rolled his eyes. "Surely you can't be so unread? To finally kill a nosferatu you must drive a stake through its heart, cut off its head, and burn it to ashes. Or just leave it out in the sun, since Hollywood has successfully dictated that we also spontaneously combust."

"And it's *true*?" Back in Chicago I'd given psycho-Vlad the full treatment out of a need to really express myself—not because I'd known it would take all that to really kill him. I felt my neck again. Clean brown hands covered my sticky pale ones. He gently pulled my hands away and tilted my head to look, like a doctor checking his work.

He smiled. "Fortunately most vampires are not fans of Buffy. We don't explode into dust at the poke of a well-placed stake or a clean slice. No, in that the old stories prevail."

"So how did you... reattach..."

"Extended propinquity works very well; I simply held your head to your neck until you decided to pull yourself together."

"Pull myself—. You did *not* just say that."

He looked confused for the first time.

"I know I spoke correctly."

Someone knocked on the kitchen door, swung it half-open.

"Is it safe in there?" the knocker asked cheerfully.

"Yes, Darren," Leroy said, smiling. "Enter freely and of your own will." I snorted; even I recognized *that* line.

The door opened the rest of the way, and I stared. *Beautiful* was not an adjective that could be applied to many men, but Darren was one of them. A tanned blond Adonis in sports shirt, casual pants and loafers, he lounged in the doorway. The cotton shirt stretched tight, showing cut but not bulky muscles; he looked like he ran instead of crunching weights at whatever country club he'd wandered away from. And I was still thirsty.

He winked at me but spoke to Leroy, and I suddenly recognized him: the guy I'd seen at Angels with my sardonic rescuer.

"The roof you sent me to was clear," he said, "so I figure their friends came back for them. But I found this." The machete he held up had blood on it. Mine? The one I chopped?

Leroy frowned. "I'd hoped to be able to talk to our attackers."

"Did you recognize them?"

"No. However, I did remain long enough to take pictures." He pulled out his cell-phone and turned the screen to me. "Do you know them, Ms. Bouchard?"

Swinging my legs off the table to scoot closer, I choked again. The screen showed two heads, set side by side. Masks off, they wore very surprised expressions.

I stopped myself from shaking my head. Cautiously rubbing my neck, I tried to ignore Darren's leaning in to look over my shoulder.

"I don't know them." I forced my hands back down, fighting the queasy conviction that my head would fall off if I turned it too far. Dammit, vampires didn't *do* that! They posed and pouted and engaged in influence-duels if they felt pissy!

And I'd thought I knew all the vamps in town from Emerson's files, not to mention the mind-numbing round of formal introductions at the Midnight Ball—the fact I didn't recognize either of them was a seriously disturbing intelligence failure. How many more unknown vamps were there?

Darren just looked cheerfully thoughtful. "I have some pull. If we photo-shop these pictures to remove evidence of their...close shaves, we may be able to enlist the help of the cops." He caught my eye and smiled sympathetically.

Leroy closed his phone. "It is nearly dawn," he said. "Ms. Bouchard? I have spoken to your grandmother, and she knows that you will be spending the day here. Darren? Will you show her to her room?"

"Sure, boss."

"Not an *imposition*, am I?" I said to his back as he disappeared through the door. Darren laughed.

"So much for Gaelic charm, right? C'mon, let's get you settled in."

Darren took me downstairs. The place had a small basement, not that common in the lower parts of New Orleans. Low-ceilinged, it felt like it had been dug out after the house was built. A steel chest in the corner large enough to hold a coffin had been bolted to the concrete walls and floor. I was willing to bet that, like my coffin, it could be locked from the inside.

"The boss had all this put in after he bought the place," he said, following the direction of my thoughts. "Kind of a secure guest-crypt, you know?" He rapped on the steel door that separated the room from the stairwell. "It's vented so you can leave after dark, but anyone trying to get in will need explosives."

The other corner held a sink and shower stall and a

wardrobe.

"There's stuff you can change into in there—just wash up first. Toss your things into the stairs and bolt the door, and you're good to go. I'll get it cleaned before night."

He left the door open a crack, and I sagged when I heard the upstairs door shut. Bolting the "crypt" door, I looked at my watch: less than ten minutes till sunrise. Spiking panic fought my creeping lethargy; blood was as good as Red Bull but I needed more than Leroy had given me if I was going to stay up much longer. Could that be why Darren hadn't offered me anything? Did they want me easy and quiet for the day? I couldn't *stay*. I needed to think, I needed to plan, but most of all I needed to be safe and not *trapped by daylight with people I didn't trust, in the middle of a fight I knew nothing about*!

I placed a text on my epad, checked to make sure I still had everything, and lifted into mist before thought could stop me.

Darren hadn't been lying about the vent; I found it by the air currents and darted out and up, to the street outside Leroy's school. The sky above me showed no stars on a brightening blue horizon. I felt thick, heavy, and fought to stay aloft as I fled west across the Quarter, every instinct screaming at me to *go back, get down, get solid! Find. A. Hole!*

There! Paul's van screeched around the corner of Chartres and Ursulines, and I dropped through the window and into the front passenger seat. Paul swore and nearly ran us up on the sidewalk. I couldn't blame him; Leroy had probably rolled my head up in his suit jacket for carrying; my face was sticky, my hair matted, and I probably looked worse than when I'd been *staked*, like a chatty homicide victim.

"Home?" He demanded, speeding up.

"No!" I gasped, nearly paralyzed at the thought of whoever had attacked tonight going through Grams to get to me. *Not again. Think!*

Fortunately, I hadn't left my own safety *completely* up to the DSA when I came to town. Quickly dialing a memorized number got a short response and an invitation. I told Paul where to go and scrambled into the back where he kept emergency gear, including an emergency blanket—a heavy, dense blanket good for smothering fires or warming an accident victim, or for keeping the sun off a vamp. Wrapping up and curling into a ball, I lay between the seats and pulled the blanket over my head.

The killer was *direct* sunlight; even filtered it burned like a blowtorch, but reflected sunlight was fine. Paul took a corner nearly on two wheels as I tried not to remember the last time I'd been caught out unprotected and in the open by daybreak. I'd spent the day curled up under a rooftop air conditioning unit, killing sunlight inches from my fingertips, a slip away from the worst sunburn ever.

The top of the blanket warmed and my skin crawled. I focused on the turns and stops, and knew when Paul turned west on Dumaine. His hard right turn slid me to the side and I heard the faster traffic that had to be North Rampart. Left on Ursuline's, and we were out of the

Quarter and into Tremé. Right, *much* slower and I heard bright laughter, happy kids on their way to school. Right again, almost there...

A bump as Paul turned off the street, and the school sounds died a little. Finally thinking ahead again, I scrubbed my face against the blanket—not that it would help—as the van came to a stop.

Lifting a corner of the blanket, I saw only shaded light. Paul opened the door as I sat up. He wasn't alone.

He'd parked us right where I'd told him to: in the narrow carriageway between St. Augustine and the new St. Augustine's Parochial School. The stern priest standing beside him looked down at me.

"Ms. Bouchard?" he asked in a thick German accent and absolutely no acknowledgement of my axe-victim appearance.

I nodded. "Father Graff? I—"

He shook his head, extending his hand. "Inside, *mein kinde*," he said. I pulled the blanket around me like a cloak and let him help me out of the van. Paul slid the door closed after me and followed.

It was hard to believe that Father Graff and the Chicago Sentinels' team chaplain were men of the same cloth; where Father Nolan was short and, well, comfortably spherical and almost always smiling, Father Graff only smiled when he remembered to and he looked stretched out and tough, a veteran of service in sunbaked countries where a low-calorie diet wasn't always optional. His close-cut dark hair was only just going grey but he had short parallel lines of white hair above one ear, the kind of streaks that usually meant old scalp wounds. He looked like the kind of shepherd prepared to violently defend his flock.

When the DSA had asked me to insert myself into New Orleans' vamp community, I'd given it some thought and called Father Nolan, asked if he knew anybody in the Big Easy. He spoke to Father Graff and arranged for my emergency gear to be sent down before I got here. I hadn't expected trouble, but after years of Extreme Contingency Planning, having a bolt-hole and an extra stash was second nature; I had *five* scattered around Chicago, and the Sentinels only knew about the one in my family home's basement.

The father took us into the small building standing at the end of the drive—the Archives Building, recently built from the shell of the church's old carriage house. The main room was windowless but big and open, a mini-museum with framed historic artifacts on the white-plastered walls and under glass in a central display cabinet. A row of computer and microfilm stations stood along one wall. An artificially backlit stained glass window with a rack for votary candles beneath—depicting St. Augustine, I presumed—took up another wall. The opposite wall held an unadorned iron cross, probably connected with the Tomb of the Unknown Slave outside.

Father Graff watched me closely, nodding when I didn't recoil from the cross.

"Father Nolan tells me you're one of the *beati*

mortus," he said.

Beati mortus: the blessed dead. Father Nolan had called me that before—his way of assuring me I still had a soul, I'd thought. Father Graff said it like it meant something more.

"I don't fear the symbols of God, father, if that's what you mean."

He shrugged. "Most monsters are men," he said, turning the deadbolt on the outside door. He gave Paul a smile too grim to be reassuring. "And you, *mein sohn*? Are you also comfortable here?"

We both started.

"Father—" Paul stuttered, and the priest shook his head.

"You may relax, *mein sohn*. It is simply that those of us who need to know, know of your gift."

"Who *are* you?"

"Currently? I am an assistant priest and the school's athletic director. More to the point, I am a *consultor* for the Congregation for the Doctrine of the Faith."

I blinked. "The what now?"

"The Holy Inquisition."

Chapter Eight

"Too dumb to live" is not a character judgement—it's an act of Darwinism.

The Artemis Files

I nearly drew my Kel-Tec—three bullets left—on a priest. Paul leaped backwards, like the man had, I don't know, *turned into a wolf* right in front of us.

Father Graff chuckled. "I am sorry. I do enjoy a little fun, and I don't get to do that very often. If the schoolchildren knew my true office, perhaps they would be a little more respectful to their athletic director."

He dropped his smile and waved us towards the computer-station chairs. Neither of us took him up on it.

"The chief role of the CDF is, and has always been, maintaining priestly discipline and doctrinal conformity within the ranks of the Church," he said. "Historically, we have also prosecuted heresy—which has famously included witchcraft."

His academic tone wasn't making me any calmer, and he sighed, looking tired.

"Contrary to what most people think they know," he continued patiently, "the office of the Inquisition did not burn millions of accused witches during the centuries of European witch-hunts. Most convicted witches were accused by their neighbors, for things like the 'evil eye' that caused cattle to sicken, crops to wither, and mothers to miscarry, and were tried and executed by their local magistrates or lords. Where the Inquisitorial Courts became involved, they were *much* more careful; most accusations of witchcraft were dismissed, and those that were upheld usually resulted in only penance or excommunication."

He gave us a moment to respond, continuing when we didn't.

"My last post was in Albania and the Balkans. Troubled breakthroughs can suffer tremendously at the hands of well-meaning but fearfully superstitious laity, but sometimes I have been called to defend the faithful from breakthrough-spawned witchcraft and sorcery. I have become something of an expert in dealing with superstitions made real."

"Given that," he watched me closely, "I'm sure you can imagine why I was sent to New Orleans?"

"Grams," I said coldly.

"The estimable Marie Bouchard, and many others. *Voodoun*—and its more...folk-magic forms when either is used for ill. And I do my best to combat the natural impulse of many of the faithful to turn to folk-religion— saint's medals used as magic talismans, blessed candles for charms. Keeping holy water in the font is a chore."

"But the *Inquisition*?" Paul finally managed to say the word. The old priest ignored him, studying me with eyes that said quite clearly that his *Boss* might wait to separate the sheep from the goats until the end, but if he himself had been commanded to give me the benefit of the doubt till then, it was a thin benefit.

And, Father Nolan's recommendation aside, he hadn't decided I wasn't a wolf yet.

"We had best get you safe for the day, *mein kinde*," he said, stepping past me.

The storage room he took us into was close and cramped, lit by just one bulb. Father Graff pulled on a back shelf, which turned out to be sitting on low casters. Behind it and the fake wall it was attached to, the storage room was deeper than it looked.

It had no amenities, just a cot, a small table and camp-light, and my emergency stash.

"The shelf latches," he said, showing me the lock opposite the hinges he'd installed. "You can pull it flush to the walls and nobody will enter until you unbolt it."

"Thank you," I said. "I'll find another place as quick as I can."

"I'll bring you water and towels," he said, and left.

Paul watched him go. "Is it me, or were you waiting for him to click his heels and give a Nazi salute? I hate this."

"I'll be safe, Paul," I said, not so sure but too tired to care anymore. Father Nolan had vouched for him and sent him my stuff to keep; whatever was going on, I trusted the Sentinels' funny little priest.

Paul had to leave it at that. "So are you going to tell me why I didn't take you home?"

Because I'm not losing family again.

"Because vampires have minions, Paul, and I'm not leading them back where they can find me in the daytime. You know what a sleeping vampire is? A *corpse*. Paul? Could you arrange a protection detail for Grams? If you have some friends willing to pull off-duty hours, I can pay. And could you dig up everything you can on Leroy? Quietly. I'll explain everything tonight, after I've found a new hole. Okay?"

He looked at me funny, but shrugged. "Okay. Call for a pick-up, chèr. I'll let your grandmère know you're safe, take care of everything. " Then he was gone, too. I pulled the shelf back, closed the latches, and sank down on the cot to wait for Father Graff to come back.

*Damn, damn, damn, damn, **damn**!*

With everything I'd learned from Blackstone, I'd *still* screwed up by the numbers. Closing my eyes, I stared at the dark inside my lids.

I'd learned damn-all, really, about the Big Easy and vampire society before I got here, and not much since— certainly no more than I'd thought I needed for my job. Worse, I'd completely failed to appreciate the physical threat someone *else* with my abilities posed if they decided to get nasty. But I'd been the only vamp in Chicago, and just couldn't take the goth posers of New Orleans seriously. I'd thought Psycho Vlad had been the nut-job serial killer exception; the rest acted like exactly what you'd expect from anyone whose breakthrough came from an obsession with a kinky romantic stereotype. But that was no excuse.

I'd been treating my stay in the Big Easy like a working vacation, and it had nearly killed me. Permanently. Doing low-risk undercover work for the local police while mapping out the vampire "underworld" for the DSA had seemed an easy price to pay for a new identity and the opportunity to get to know my Bouchard family and roots, even if playing to the whole Fiend of The Night stereotype made me want to vomit. The few precautions I'd taken had been out of habit.

And let's face it—I never wanted to know about my "condition." Get my supply of liquid iron, stay out of sunlight, don't think about it.

I'd finished whipping myself by the time Father Graff returned, and after he left and I locked myself in again I was barely able to clean up and change into the spare clothes in my pack before collapsing back onto the cot. Before I gave in entirely I managed to call Grams' phone, leave a message. For nearly two months—since learning of each other's existence, really—we'd lived in the same house like two cats sharing a territory. She'd accommodated me into her life with barely a ripple, and I still didn't know what we *were* yet, but we were family. If she'd woken up to find I hadn't checked in, no idea where I was... Paul wouldn't be able to run fast enough.

Turning off the camp light, I dropped into bottomless sleep.

Drunks are easy. They also taste terrible.

When night fell I woke up so thirsty I could hardly see straight. After texting Mr. Gray to set up a meeting (it would probably be the low point of my night) and unlatched the shelving so Father Graff could get in, I rose into mist right through the ceiling, unwilling to risk meeting anyone I knew. At every twitch of wind, I half-expected to feel other vamps searching the night for me.

In my first nights hunting for myself in Chicago, before I'd gotten a fake driver's license good enough to get me into the clubs and pick-up bars, I'd had to find prey on the streets. Give me a minute of good eye contact and a few words and I can enthrall anyone, but the pace is faster in a street encounter; when you've got seconds, only a will weakened by drugs or alcohol will fold fast enough.

I'd scouted Tremé when I first arrived in town. Separated from the Quarter by Rampart Street, it had been the home of free blacks and dark Creoles from before Louisiana became a state (St. Augustine was the oldest African-American Catholic parish in the country). It was mostly residential, though, and the best place I'd found was the Candlelight Lounge. A local hangout except on Wednesday nights when the Tremé Brass Band played and tourists flocked to catch that good Big Easy sound, it sat on a dark and quiet street backed by Interstate Ten. It served beans and rice and cheap alcohol, and had just what I wanted.

I was way too white to be unnoticeable, and so thirsty anyone I talked to would feel like he was being stared at by a starving lioness waiting for him to twitch before she brought him down, so I needed prey that was already separated from the herd. Early patrons had parked their cars along the street, and I made my first choice a rebuilt Chevy with tinted windows that made the interior perfectly private.

Watching the lounge from the roof of the two story home across the street, I waited until a lone patron stepped out, walking unsteadily. He wove his careful way down the sidewalk, fumbled keys out of his pocket, and attacked the door of the rusty and beat-up pickup truck beside the Chevy. *Close enough.* I dove into mist and swooped low over the street.

He managed to get his door open and I flowed in around him, catching him mid-heave as he pulled himself in and slammed the door. He jerked as I pulled myself together on the passenger's side, but before his pickled brain had time to realize the danger I'd grabbed his head and yanked us both face-down below the level of the dashboard, me on top of him.

He found himself staring at the stick shift while I whispered in his ear.

"Shhh. Shhh. It's okay," I told him, hitting him with all the influence I could muster in my thirsty state. He relaxed, just like that, breathing slowly as I held his shoulders to keep him from slipping right off the car seat and to the floor of the driver's space. Pulling down the back of his collar to expose his neck, I bit.

It didn't matter that he'd been doing heavy labor somewhere today and hadn't bathed, or that his blood tasted like he'd chugged wood-alcohol. I forced myself to count, to stop at thirty, stayed crouched over him shivering with my thirst for *more*. Through it all the insects outside made more noise than we did.

I finally raised my head and scanned the street, listening to his quiet breathing. "Upsy-daisy now," I said softly, pulling him back upright behind the steering wheel. He'd dropped his keys by his feet, and I retrieved them. His head flopped back and he rolled his eyes to look at me, smiling sleepily. Pulling a fifty out of my pocket, I handed it to him with the keys.

"Here's what you're going to do. Listening?" He nodded loosely and I held his chin, keeping our gazes locked.

"You're going to sit here thinking about how nice it is to be going home. Okay? You're going to decide you're too drunk, you're going to go back inside, and you're going to call a cab. You're not going to remember anything about tonight, and tomorrow you're going to check out Alcoholics Anonymous. Got it?"

He nodded again, like a tired but happy puppy, and I patted him on the shoulder. Opening the passenger window a crack, I lifted into mist and away. He would blank on the night—I was confident of that. My final suggestion *might* stick, and was the most I could give for what I took.

I found two more donors before I felt on top again: the second (a cabby) took me to my third (a tourist bar and a player looking for a hookup). From there I walked back to St. Augustine, achingly alert for shadowers on the wind. Paul waited for me in the dark carriageway, leaning against the van, hands in his pockets.

"Now are we going to talk?" he asked, straightening.

"I haven't got a new place, yet. I had to top up."

He scowled darkly. "What did you do, chèr?"

"A drunk, a cabbie, and a player," I said tonelessly. "The drunk got home safe, the cabbie got a big tip, and the player thinks he got lucky. And I'm as full as a happy tick."

"Jacky—"

"I can't hit the regular clubs, Paul. Or Sable's. I don't want to see another vamp except on my terms until I know who wants me permanently dead." *Which gives me just until the Midnight Ball to figure out what's going on. Crap.* "Help me pack? And I need you to take me shopping. I've got to *accessorize.*"

"Jacky, what is going on?"

"Please."

He stood there for a long moment, then slumped, defeated.

"I'll help you tonight, me. But then, chèr, we're done unless you can tell me you're still on the side of the angels."

"I want to know, as well," Leroy said behind me.

"*Jesus H. Christ!*" Paul's gun was in his hand—a 9mm SIG-Sauer that wouldn't do much against a charging vampire.

"You may relax, Detective Negri. I only seek information." Leroy stepped out of the shadows behind the van. He wore a grey-black suit and shirt, black tie, no jewelry or bright buttons anywhere—talk about GQ-camouflage.

Realizing I'd drawn my own useless Kel-Tec, I put it away and swallowed a *How did you find me?* He hadn't; he'd found Paul.

"I believe we should go somewhere less exposed to talk," he said.

"Inside will be fine, *Herr* Leroy."

Father Graff stepped around the side of a beat-up pickup truck I'd seen earlier tonight. The shotgun he carried looked much more effective.

"Is anybody else out there?" I said loudly. " 'cause now would be a good time."

Chapter Nine

Never argue with a priest with a gun; he's protecting someone or he's on a mission from God—either way he won't hesitate to send you to Jesus.

Jacky Bouchard, *The Artemis Files*

A vampire, a werewolf, and a priest walk into a bar. What a perfect joke, spoiled only by the extra vampire (me), and the fact that we were walking into a church. Well, the Archive Building. I shook my head; my homogoblin— *hemoglobin*—high hadn't passed yet. Le-*roy* was the odd vamp out tonight. What the hell did he want?

Father Graff went in ahead, taking a moment before formally inviting us (Leroy, really) inside. I saw that he had covered the section of wall holding the iron cross with a light screen, one he could pull down quick if necessary.

So, he didn't trust Leroy either. I hid a smirk, blood-infused mood swinging up; Father Graff seemed more likely to use the shotgun than a cross. *What does he load it with? Must ask later.*

The priest set his weapon down on the document-viewing table in the center of the room, facing us across it.

"Ms. Bouchard," he said with European formality. "Before we go any further together, I need to hear about Andy."

Andy? Andy was handy. *Stop that.* Even Leroy was viewing me with alarm. I crossed my arms, tried to look as serious as the situation was. I was never doing three in one night *again.*

"Andy is the owner of the truck outside, father?"

He nodded.

"I lost a lot of blood last night—you saw me wearing most of it."

He nodded again.

"I—and Mr. Leroy—were attacked by vampires. One of them killed me; if not for Leroy I would be ashes on a Bourbon Street rooftop now and tonight I needed to feed, badly. I can't go near my normal territory until I know who attacked us and why."

"So you attacked a member of my parish after receiving sanctuary—"

"Father, *please.*" My mood had absolutely bottomed, and I carefully kept my eyes off him. I would *not* influence him, or give him reason to think I was. "There are two ways for me to get what I need—force or consent. I couldn't get consent tonight, not anywhere safe. Andy is alright?"

"Yes." I could feel Father Graff's gaze on me.

"He shouldn't have remembered anything, father. How did he..."

"He walked back into the bar waving a fifty and asking for a cab. Johnny Good knew something had happened when he started going on about an angel and finding an AA meeting. When he passed out, Johnny found the bite marks and brought him to me."

I closed my eyes. "I should have told him to sleep it off in the truck."

"Why didn't you?"

Why didn't I? "Tremé can be a little rough at night." I winced when Paul choked, remembering his attitude towards my hobby of making things less predictable for New Orleans' human predators. In the silence, I risked a glance at Father Graff. He looked...like he didn't know what he was looking at.

"So you stalked a member of my flock," he said slowly. "You enslaved his will, drank his blood, then gave him fifty dollars and *commanded* him to take a cab home and go to an Alcoholics Anonymous meeting?"

Now Leroy was trying very hard not to laugh. With all the blood I'd taken in, I felt a blush climbing my face.

"Yes, father," I managed.

He pinched the bridge of his nose. "I am grateful you are not Catholic, *mein kinde*," he said with a groan. "I would need a Jesuit to decide on your penance."

"Why a fifty?" Paul asked. "That's more than a local cab."

I sighed. "It's the going rate for a blood-bank donation."

Leroy completely lost it.

I promised Father Graff I'd be gone before morning. Since I wasn't actually asking for the protection of the church this was all just a sideline to him, and, really I could understand why he didn't want us around; vampires might not be a problem to church *doctrine*, but the fantasy and addiction we created and fed from had to represent a danger to his flock. *Beati mortus* or not, this wasn't the place for me.

Whatever his feelings, he accepted my apology for Andy, and departed after getting my promise to lock up as we left. It was all very civilized.

"A most interesting clergyman," Leroy commented as the door closed behind him.

"I think he has a secret lair somewhere," I said. "Or at least a ring of informants. He knew all about—" I shut up.

"All about Paul?" Leroy supplied. "Or what the two of you really do together?"

Paul *growled*, and he held up a hand. In the light reflecting from the historical displays, he was all shadows, dark, dangerous, and amused.

"Be calm, Detective Negri," he said. "After Jacqueline informed me that she didn't belong to Sable's court, I had Darren look around a little. He is well connected, very useful, and since I do not drink from children I can hardly object to your activities. I merely came here tonight to ensure that Jacqueline was unharmed after her…adventures. And to learn what she wished to speak to me about last night."

He looked completely calm himself, despite the fact that his sword-cane probably wasn't silver and in his wolfman form Paul could probably rip his head off. I had a sudden vision of Paul doing just that to make sure Leroy came along quietly. He could always put him back together at the precinct…

If Leroy thought he was a suspect in any way, he didn't show it. I bought time by filling Paul in on the details of last night's attack, relieved that he understood why I wasn't reporting it; cop or not, Paul was still a bayou boy from Church Pointe, and he knew all about taking care of trouble inside the family.

He did demand that Leroy send him the "head shots" he'd taken of two of our attackers.

"That will not be a problem, detective," Leroy said, neglecting to mention he'd planned on having Darren call in a favor to do just that. "In return, I would appreciate it if you would tell me what Jacqueline hasn't. What did she want to speak to me about?"

"She was looking for a date?" Paul shot back and I sputtered. "I just watch her back while we do our thing."

"You don't watch it well, Detective Negri. Darren informed me of the hunters."

"Hey—" I started, wondering just how deep the leaks in Paul's department ran.

"Considering she got *beheaded* out with you—"

"Paul! Stop! You guys are fighting over keeping *me*

safe? Seriously?" More blood inside me meant more "living" reactions, and I was so mad my hands shook. "I swear to God I'll shoot the next one who acts like I'm some freaking damsel in distress!"

Paul and Leroy shared a *look* and I almost screamed.

"What did you come to see me about?" Leroy asked. To shut him up, I told him about Acacia and what the hunters had been trying to accomplish.

He was silent when I finished.

"Acacia."

"Yes," I said.

"And your lieutenant thinks that she was unintentionally turned?"

Paul nodded and I kept my mouth shut. Sometimes I wondered if vamps were mildly psychic as well; Leroy's eyes said he knew I wasn't sharing everything.

"This may explain a great deal," he said finally. "Detective Negri, what do you know about V-Juice?"

"What?" Paul said, and I echoed him.

"Your department really should widen its focus, detective. V-Juice is 'vampire blood.' There are many aspiring vampires, and few vampires willing to risk the sire scam for any amount of money."

"Okay."

"So there is a market for V-Juice. It is pig's blood—I've tasted it—laced with a methamphetamine that makes its users feel strong, powerful. They take it believing it is vampire blood, that enough doses will turn them. Naturally they become addicted."

What?

I opened my mouth but couldn't get anything out as my world shifted again, in a direction I didn't dare trust. Paul swore. "Have there been overdoses?" he asked before I could draw breath to.

Leroy nodded.

"A few. I have been quietly trying to find the distributors, but the sellers are being careful and someone is protecting them."

"Angels, the other night?" I asked carefully.

"It is being sold there, yes."

"So what does this explain?" Paul asked.

No master vampire. Enough idiots take a nasty ride with the stuff, *somebody* trying for it was bound to turn, no sire needed.

No master vampire. I stood frozen, still as a stone gargoyle.

"Acacia, Paul," I said, voice amazingly normal. "She may not have a sire. What's more likely? That a vamp is playing the con—and how often could he do it without getting caught and could Acacia have ever paid him enough to risk it—or that she got her breakthrough off V-Juice?"

Paul bit his nail and did the math while I tried to think my way around it. The odds of a normal vamp "siring" another vamp were one in thousands. Which was why I'd been staring at the terrifying possibility of a new master vamp. But if dozens, maybe hundreds of wannabes were taking...

"So," I said. "*Acacia* comes to town looking for a vamp to turn her, chooses me, but loses her nerve? And if she was obviously a wannabe, not just a fan, somebody could have sold V-Juice to her."

Paul looked up. "But there still have to be vampires involved. Vamps attacked the two of you."

"Yes," Leroy agreed. "I have been asking around, and I am certain that because of this I was last night's target."

"Was. Now Jacky's in it too—they have to assume you've read her in. Shit."

"As you say, *merde.*"

Leroy had what he wanted to know from me, and with zero desire to stick around a church—even in its one safe room—he didn't linger. Paul wanted to take me home; he said he was working on an off-the-books safe house, but he figured he could keep me safe at Grams for at least one day. Instead I got him to take me "shopping." An hour later I stood in a duelist stance, test-firing a .50 caliber Desert Eagle with quick double taps. I'd stretched my senses all the way there, but hadn't felt any other vamps in the air. Nobody seemed to be following us, either.

Boom-boom. Boom-boom. Boom-boom.

"Nice grouping," Bobby said, taking off his ear protectors. The owner of Masson Guns and Ammo had opened his range for me as a favor to Paul.

He'd frowned when I ignored the offered ear protectors and snorted when I squared off against the targets with a one-handed grip, arm out sideways like an old time duelist instead of taking up the two-handed forward pointing Weaver stance. Now he shook his head.

"Damn, but you've got the solidest grip I've ever seen. Might as well have it clamped to a tripod—I don't think the barrel moved an inch."

I laughed. "Strength of the dead has its perks, Mr. Masson. It's easy to stay on target, and shooting two-handed means I'd have to turn my whole body instead of just my arm and head for offside shooting. Not to mention giving anyone shooting at me a broader silhouette."

"I can see that. Good. Desert Eagles are bear-stoppers, but they kick; let it ride back and you can mess up the timing of the slide and stovepipe it. Jams are bad when you're in a fight. So what bear do you want to stop with this?"

I ejected and checked the magazine, cleared the barrel. "Bloodsucking ones."

Bobby looked back at Paul, chuckled nervously. "Kidding, right?"

"Nope. Last night I shot one in the head and barely slowed him down. His buddy cut my head *off*." I sliced a finger across my throat and gave Bobby a grin, showing fang. "I figure a .50 caliber round to a leg or an arm will shatter bones, slow him down a little. A shot to the neck might decapitate him. I'll take two of these."

Bobby brought out a second Desert Eagle and together we stripped and checked both of them. I'd asked Paul to take me to a *gunsmith*, and he had; Bobby knew his stuff. He used tape and blue paper to get my hand measurements and promised to have one fitted for my grip by tomorrow night—then I could trade and get the second gun done. He also offered to stiffen the trigger pull to match my strength.

When I asked for fitted micro laser-sights and beveled magazine wells for smoother reloads and started in on ammunition options, he laughed. "Where did you train? Special Ops?"

I smiled. "Close," I said, thinking of Sam, the retired Navy Seal range master who taught me the full tactical shooter course—cold, hot, and dynamic range work.

"Okay, don't tell me," Bobby said when I didn't elaborate. "So what else do we need?" He fitted me with a shoulder holster stripped for speed drawing and able to carry a couple of spare magazines, threw in a full maintenance kit, and I remembered to ask about knives. He found me a pair of Arkansas toothpicks—thirteen inches of double-edged straight blade goodness. "Should I be concerned?" he asked, ringing everything up.

I looked at his worried face and gave his question the seriousness it deserved.

"I don't think so," I said. "Just a little vamp-on-vamp violence. Hopefully it will never hit the news."

"Should I stock up on stakes and stuff?"

"Stakes are Hollywood. You know how hard it is to push a pointed piece of wood through someone's ribcage? And the heart's a pretty small target." Paul coughed behind me. Okay, I was starting to sound like a vampire serial-killer.

"Seriously Bobby," he said. My unexpected expertise

obviously bugged him, but now he was trying not to laugh. "Crosses, holy water—jus' make sure it's the real stuff—but like Jacky said, it's family business you know? Wouldn't worry about it, me."

Looking at Paul, I realized I was hosed. All we had to worry about was a new drug ring that might be creating accidental vampires, *if we were lucky*. But only I knew the real nightmare scenario and that wasn't fair. Ignorance could get him killed. I had to read him in on master vampires and supervamps, everything. And I had to introduce him to Artemis. He wasn't going to take it well.

But everyone else was going to meet Artemis, too. They weren't going to take it any better.

Chapter Ten

The thing to remember about a vampire is, it's a corpse. *An animated corpse, you bet. Well preserved? Absolutely. But cadaver-dogs can tell the difference; they can smell that so-subtle tang of cellular necrosis, and it bugs the hell out of them to see a vampire moving. People can tell, too, if they know what to look for: room-temperature handshake, milky complexion, a spooky absence of all the ticks and twitches of a body busy living. So where's the best place to hide a corpse?*

Jacky Bouchard, *The Artemis Tapes*

Paul dropped me off on Chartres Street; he didn't want to, but he knew about my DSA connection and knew he wasn't going to meet him. Gray preferred meeting at Napoleon House because the old bar on the corner of Chartres and St. Louis was a historical site and tourist hangout—the overworked staff saw *lots* of new faces every night, making regulars stand out in the crowd. And he wanted to stand out.

Gray always looked like a seedy lawyer or corrupt councilman out to relax, an image strengthened by the Pimm's Cup—a lemonade cocktail and Napoleon House's signature drink—that he held in his hand as he read the paper. Seeing me, he put down the drink and took another bite of his muffaletta before wiping his hand and winking at me.

One of the fey (do *not* call them fairies unless they're three inches tall with wings), Gray had held down the DSA's New Orleans station for years. I had no idea why he wasn't in San Francisco where the Seelie Court hung out in their perpetual Ren-Faire.

"Hey, darlin'" he said. "Don't be shy—Kimie knows to leave us alone." He'd grabbed a corner table, and looked a perfect match for the crumbling plaster walls hung with old pictures and yellowing framed newspaper clippings. Glancing back at the bar as I sat, I caught "Kimie" glaring at us.

I raised an eyebrow. "How nasty were you? Did she spit in your sandwich?"

He grinned, leaning close. "Believe me, I checked. If she spit in my drink, the alcohol took care of it." His hand crept over to cover mine and he squeezed. When I winced for our audience and pulled away he sighed and sat back, looking mulish. He waved Kimie over.

"Another Pimm's for my girl. She needs sweetening up." Kimie actually hesitated and I looked away, quiet and trapped, till she came back with the drink—and an iced water glass and pitcher—and retreated again. My "date" chuckled.

"Make sure I'm wearing that when you leave."

"That won't be a problem."

"Hey darlin', don' be like that. I was starting to wonder, you being involved in a police incident an' all. Makes a man wonder what he isn't hearing about."

His hand came back to play with mine, and I let a shudder out for Kimie's benefit. The man was good at his role; his voice made me want to disinfect, but his eyes were cold. The guy ran the DSA's New Orleans station for a reason, and it wasn't just because his fey glamour kept anyone from remembering details he didn't want them to. I had no idea how he did it but it wasn't telepathy; it even worked on me, and I was brain dead with no sparking neurons to affect. *I* only saw his pointy ears when I focused, and they never showed up in photographs. Magic.

A fanatic about details, he used our meetings to strengthen his cover as an amoral "fixer" who could buy anything and do anything for a price. They *always* remembered Gray—and remembered me as a mousy worn down blonde "girlfriend" he bullied and bought drinks for. They probably thought I *did things* for him.

In low tones and trying to look like I was telling something shameful, I sketched out Emerson's theory, the second attack, and Leroy's revelations. His expression didn't change.

"So, you think someone's found a new hit-and-miss way of making vamps?" He hadn't missed the fact that, Acacia aside, there were at least two vamps I didn't know in town. "Building himself a bloodsucker army? Why?"

"I don't know, but three or four isn't an army yet. I want him before Emerson gets to him—news of vamps being made by drugs is almost as bad as the real thing."

"Does Emerson know?"

"If he didn't, Paul will tell him. And Emerson's good at his job. What do you want me to do?" I crossed my fingers beneath the table.

"Exactly what you're going to do. Find this sonovabitch. Find out what he *is*, if he's the real deal or a good imitation. But don't take too long; this'll go up the chain, and they're cautious at the top—without hard facts, they'll go with Better Safe Than Sorry." He shrugged, unconcerned. "Now get out."

I skimmed condensation from my water glass and wiped my cheeks to wet them, tossed my drink in his face, and slapped him for good measure. Twice. It was the most fun I'd had all night, and Kimie stared at me in awe as I stormed past, already thinking about where I was going to spend the day.

St. Louis Cemetery #1, New Orleans' oldest necropolis, filled up before the Civil War and most of its old mausoleums were neglected and decaying. I'd recovered my gear from the church, and now I crept along the shadowed alleys between white and age-stained tombs, eying my prospects.

New Orleans' old cemeteries are not places to be after dark, unless of course you're a resident. They're famous since, unlike in cemeteries elsewhere, all their residents sleep above ground in mausoleums; they have to since the water table is so close to the grass that when it rains real hard, buried caskets just come right back up.

The moon had waned to a thin crescent, giving me welcome darkness but reminding me that the Midnight Ball was only four nights away. The cemetery's caretakers locked its gates at night, but its walls weren't high and its proximity to the Iberville Projects meant running into project kids sneaking in over the wall on an adventure was always a possibility. I'd jumped the old graveyard's wall easily enough with my stuffed bag over my shoulder.

You always see Hollywood vampires hanging around graveyards, and of course goths love them, but properly consecrated graves are *holy ground*. Since the Event, in places like New Orleans they'd gotten *really* serious about making sure graveyards were ritually blessed at least annually. Church processions through the tombs, with waving aspergillum spraying holy water and swinging thuribles fumigating with liturgical incense, were a big part of All Saint's Day now, so graveyards that hadn't been completely abandoned were the *last* place you were likely to meet a vampire; even the stupidest vamp wouldn't go where he could get a nasty burn off just leaning against the side of a tomb.

But crosses, holy water, the host, none of that bothered *me*, and the safest place to hide is where nobody thinks you can go.

I found my new home right next to a whitewashed and well-kept mausoleum belonging to the Most Sacred Order of Funny-Hatted Drinking Buddies. A big one with dozens of vaults still being used, it overshadowed an old and decrepit quadruple decker belonging to the Bacquets, a family that obviously wasn't around anymore. The top vault was dated 1873, the mausoleum's roof had fallen in on it, and its bottom two vaults had been smashed open sometime and never reclosed. The third vault, just at head-height, had been opened and bricked up. The bricks were old and blackened.

The tomb right next to it was in much better shape. I stood in its shadow for five minutes, listening to the night, and then scaled it to drop into the Bacquet's exposed top vault. Rubble filled the open space and I cleared a spot to work in, giving the night one more good listen as I assembled my field drill. The diamond bit made an easy job of the vault floor, and I worked my fiberscope into the hole. As I'd hoped, the third vault was clear, whoever had occupied it long gone.

My full bag weighed just under my carrying limit, but there was no way I could fit it in with me so I tucked it under the biggest pieces of roofing I could find, keeping out only my weapons and field gear. I went to mist and pulled myself through the quarter-inch hole and into the vault. Snug inside, I wiggled around to get the blanket and pillow under me, then stretched out and switched on the dim camp light I'd brought with me and accessed my epad for a little reading before bedtime.

Paul had sent me everything he could find on Leroy, and it was past time to do my homework. He also included a file on Acacia, but it was thin on information—family background, school records, first appearance in New Orleans as a vamp—and since Leroy was actively involved in some side of all this I was much more interested in him at the moment.

Twenty minutes later I was swearing like a sailor.

Leroy didn't exist.

He came to New Orleans already a vampire, but every known breakthrough, supernatural or otherwise, became a person of interest to governments and law enforcement; there was no way for him *not* to have a paper and electronic trail. But the French Sûreté hadn't heard of him, Interpol didn't know anything about him, and as "Marc Leroy" he had no history of residence in Orleans—or anywhere else in France.

How could he be so *French* and not be from France?

And why was he here?

Besides New Orleans being Vampire Central, of course. But if he came here for *that*, why his lack of participation in the whole vampire scene? The Midnight Ball, the occasional club appearance, that was it.

Paul's files included business and tax records, and the first time his name and tax-ID appeared on a piece of paper was when he bought his building—in full, no mortgage. He'd incorporated his fencing school two months after arriving, and he'd been a good boy since.

Between the school and his bodyguarding business, he made good money and paid his taxes without resort to shelters, offshore accounts, or other legal dodges. Personally, he was as clean as a vamp could get—no complaints, arrests, charges, Notes Of Interest. He lived behind his school with Darren, who I'd thought of as his house boy but was apparently a practicing pro bono attorney to the vamp community. Darren financed his practice through a retainer agreement with one paying client, the LH Association.

I noted that last bit for later research, and closed the useless file.

In my months of apprenticeship with the Sentinels, Blackstone had taught me to triage questions for order of importance and then to move from what I knew to what I didn't know. Now I stared at the granite slab above me.

So, what did I really know?

Start with appearance, manner, *attitude*.

The man looked *good*, handsome as sin as Grams would say. African-European—what Heather, one of my less PC high school girlfriends, would have called "light chocolate." His narrow nose, cheekbones, chin were aristocratically cut. He had clear, grey raptor's eyes.

He was *always* well groomed, but other than wearing black he didn't follow vampire fashion—not goth, punk, or noir. He didn't hunt publicly or feed off fang fans. Where did he get his donors? Were he and Darren lovers, like everyone thought Paul and I were? If they were, he still needed more than Darren could give him.

Moving on, his attitude towards the rest of the vamp community was... *disdain*. He didn't enjoy the posing any more than I did, he despised Sable, he—

My thoughts skidded to a stop and I nearly bashed my head trying to sit up.

He was *me*.

Oh *crap*.

I'd forgotten that Marie Laveau's tomb could be a busy place at night, and the tourists woke me not long after sunset. I checked my watch to be certain the sun had truly hit the horizon, then misted up into the top vault to spy.

Blue still touched the western sky, but stars were coming out and the shadows had disappeared into night. The guide led the noisy group with a camp lantern— everyone else had little club lightsticks—and I remembered hearing that they'd recently begun funding historic restorations by conducting "voodoo tours." They couldn't keep them out, so why not take advantage and minimize the damage? I quickly packed my stuff, but then temptation won and I followed them, floating through the alleys to the famous voodoo queen's grave. Halfway there I reformed and quietly joined the back of the group.

The guide slipped in a pretty good history lesson along their indirect rout, about how most of the residents of the cemetery were pre-Civil War and had died of yellow fever. He talked about other famous residents and about preservation efforts, and the group pretty much tuned him out. The tomb of New Orlean's most famous voodoo queen looked worn but cared for, a whitewashed narrow three-vault stack with no indication of which one she was in. Recent visitors had covered the ground in front of it with offerings: coins, beads, flowers, candles—even shot-glasses filled with whisky. The guide turned off his camp light to leave the tomb lit by candlelight, and as the group crowded forward to take pictures or leave their own offerings with wishes for love, fortune, and darker things, my inner devil began pushing me.

After five years of hunting I could read a group like nobody's business, and I easily picked out the bored, the tagalongs, and the nicotine-fiends. I tapped the guy next to me on the shoulder.

"I'm dying here, got a smoke?" I whispered, giving him my best smile and pushing just a little influence at him. His pupils widened and he grinned. "Sure!" He fumbled in his pockets, found his pack and lighter while the girl beside him snapped pictures of the tomb.

When he lit me up she turned, realizing something was going on. Taking a drag, I exhaled with a sigh.

"Thanks," I sighed. "I'd have killed for a cig." Then I misted quick, dropping the cigarette and pulling into the shadows before they could blink. He screamed, she screamed, and I flowed around the crowd to snuff all the candles in passing, floating away as the shouts and screams spread behind me.

I was still laughing when Paul picked me up in a classic Cadi. I'd gone back for my things and still gotten out faster than the tourists, who'd scattered through the cemetery.

One of the speeding tour vans had nearly hit me on the street.

"What?" I asked when he looked at me.

"Do I want to know?"

"Probably not, but if you hear a new ghost story about Marie Laveau's grave, it wasn't me."

"We need to talk," he said, checking his mirrors. "Someone made a try for you today, *chèr*. Mama Marie got in his way."

Chapter Eleven

I hate a lot of people, on general principle.

Jacky Bouchard, *The Artemis Files.*

"Turn around!" I screamed. Paul was *not* headed for Esplanade.

"She's not home!" he said quickly. "She's down at the precinct having words with Emerson, and we're not going there. It's bad for our cover."

The precinct. Thank God not the hospital. Or the morgue. I had to remind myself to breathe so I could speak.

"What happened?"

"Somebody sent a professional, *chèr.* A big guy armed with every anti-vampire tool in the box: crosses, holy water, stakes, butcher's knife, lots of fire-starter. He went in maybe an hour before sunset, relied on how deeply you guys sleep to take you in your coffin, I guess."

My nails were digging divots in my palms. "How did he get past the guys you had watching?"

"I'm going to find out. Oz and Steve are two of the best. Anyway, he never made it up to your room; your grandmother was there with a client."

"And?" I pushed when he stopped.

"*Chèr*... The hitter brought a gun for them. Your grandmother says it jammed when he tried to shoot her. So he pulled the butcher's knife and... he tripped over Legba and fell on it. Dead before we got there."

"You're jok—"

"Jacky, your grandmère has the *mojo*! You've been living with her for weeks and you still haven't figured that out? This guy had to be from out of town; *nobody* local would take a contract out that meant crossing Mama Marie..."

Paul's voice muted to a background buzz as murder rose inside me like a tide of rotten blood. Whoever had sent a killer into Gram's house was going to scream when I found him. It was all I could do to keep from misting away. I really, *really* wanted to get into the morgue and seriously desecrate a corpse after draining it dry.

Sickened, I dropped my head back against the seat and closed my eyes, tasting blood in my mouth; I'd bitten myself when I screamed at Paul. If the hitter hadn't been dead, nobody could have stopped me from killing him.

Paul stopped talking and looked over at me. "Are you alright?"

"No," I croaked. "I need you to take me to church."

Not what he'd been expecting, and he was even more surprised when I told him which one. As he drove down narrow streets watching his mirror for tails, I called Grams. No details, just *I'm with Paul and alright.* She threatened Paul, he made respectful promises, his fingers white on the steering wheel, and I kept quiet. It all felt deeply wrong.

Parking was a bitch this close to Mardi Gras, but Paul found us a spot a couple of streets from Jackson Square and we walked. I wore my jacket to hide my new gun and knife—again glad I didn't sweat—and we wound our way through the happy tourists and partiers, past a jazz band performing in front of General Jackson's statue. As white as the cemetery tombs, St. Louis Cathedral looked across Chartres Street to the square. Not well lit, its shadowed mass rose above the street lamps to frown disapprovingly at the frivolity displayed in front of it.

The cathedral remained open after sunset, for the gift shop and for those who wanted to come inside and pray. Paul dipped his fingers in the font at the entrance and crossed himself before remembering me, then frowned when I did the same. Not that I was confirmed Catholic— growing up, my family had been Sunday Baptists and not much stuck, but I preferred to be inside a house of God for the talk Paul and I were about to have.

Right now any reassurance that I remained *beati mortus* helped.

The place was almost empty, and we chose a pew facing the shrine of the Holy Mother at the front of the left gallery. Paul lit a candle and said a prayer, and I lit one too for Grams. I wanted to *see* her, and that wasn't going to happen until the current situation was resolved. We sat far away from the closest visitor, who sat in front of the sanctuary with rosary in hand, reciting from a prayer book. As long as we were quiet we'd be invisible to him.

"What if somebody recognizes you here?" Paul asked.

I smiled thinly, sitting so I could keep an eye out. "I'm using a little influence—anybody seeing me in a church will think I *can't* be here, so they'll realize I'm someone else. It's a simple I'm Not Here suggestion."

"Could you make *me* think you're not here?"

I ignored the implied *have you*? "Not anymore, and not if you were looking for me."

He nodded. "*Chèr*, I talked to Emerson before the call came in on Mama Marie. Leroy was right about the V-Juice, and Emerson's already got teams watching Acacia and Belladonna. We didn't hear about it because he likes to compartmentalize, but I've got a file of overdose cases—they found a whole bunch stashed together. I'll send you the file, see if you recognize any of them...and why don't you look happier about that?"

"Because whatever side Leroy's on," I said, carefully looking away, "there's something you need to know about him. And about me."

I set aside my fears for Grams and told Paul about Tommy Walker, the goth nerd of my high school. He'd been invisible to It Girls like me despite the dark eye makeup, the black clothes, and the hostile attitude he'd used to scream his indifference. I'd never been mean to the freaks—or even really noticed them—and he'd never been insane enough to ask out a cheerleader, but he'd noticed me. Apparently a lot.

Everyone says that hindsight is 20/20, but that's crap; after five years I still couldn't remember doing anything to make him fixate on me, or any warning that he had. No black roses left at my locker, no love letters in calligraphy, no *Bela Lugosi's Dead* mix CD, nothing.

Paul didn't say a word while I told him about Tommy's going deep vampire-goth after graduation, joining a vampire "coven," getting fang caps, and finally committing suicide. Tommy opened his veins in the middle of a pentagram while I was in the middle of my sophomore year at community college. In a better world he would have bled out and died; instead he got exactly what he'd hoped for—his obsession-triggered breakthrough into true vampirehood.

All that was normal in my world now, and I could see Paul wasn't following me; most vamps were obsessive goths or vampire-romance lovers who turned through suicide or misadventure. Then I told him about how dead Tommy, risen as psycho-Vlad, tricked his way into our home and ripped my parent's throats out while I hid screaming in a closet. How he kidnapped me and locked me in a basement hole for two weeks while he fed off me and enthralled me over and over again until I loved him so deep and mindlessly I'd have killed my own parents if he'd asked. Til all I'd wanted was his bite. And how he'd killed me.

Paul finally got it. "*Chèr*—dear God in Heaven. You're *progeny*? What happened to—"

I laughed woodenly. "Staked, burned, ashes scattered on Lake Michigan. So now you know why I don't like other vamps much."

"And you still think Acacia may have a sire?"

"Maybe. But Marc Leroy definitely has one." I told him about super-vamps, watched him try and wrap his mind around the idea of a whole class of vampire not hung up on holy objects and other compulsions.

"You're *sure* about Leroy?"

"He didn't flinch at entering a church, and wasn't even a little worried about what Father Graff could do to him. He doesn't *like* the vamp-scene, not even a bit. His place, the part of it I saw, doesn't have a trace of goth, and he's got that whole I'm Too Cool To Be A Vampire thing going. He works for a living! There's no way he turned the usual way."

I didn't point out that Leroy was black, and black goths were as rare as...well, I'd never seen one, and that he was good looking as hell. I could easily imagine a vamp fixating on him like psycho-Vlad had on me.

"Do you think he got turned accidentally? Like Emerson was thinking with Acacia?"

"Maybe. But there's one more thing, and you've got to swear this doesn't go back to Emerson or anyone else official." I looked away again so he'd know I wasn't trying to influence him.

"Okay," he said finally. "As long as it's not a crime I'd have to report."

So I told him all about Artemis and master vampires and Killing Nights.

Chapter Twelve

The bats have left the bell tower,
The victims have been bled.
Red velvet lines the black box,
Bela Lugosi's dead.
Undead undead undead.

Nouvelle Vague, *Bela Lugosi's Dead.*

Not *the* Killing Nights of course, the ones that never happened now. Just the possibility. Take one psycho master vamp, he enthralls and turns three or four dozen, at least one of those is now a master vamp too and completely under his control... Bite and repeat for the ultimate undead pyramid scheme, each sire loyal to the one above him and controlling a couple more, and most of their covens full of fanatically loyal supervamps with almost zero vampire weaknesses. All hail the vampire apocalypse.

Even the possibility was bad enough for me; *any* master vamps I found were getting recycled into the Mississippi. If Acacia or Leroy had a sire, he was ashes headed for the sea as soon as I got to him.

Paul must have read something in my eyes; he shook off the news of my former vigilante status and visions of burning cities, and frowned.

"Okay," he said. "I'll buy that some vampires are made—that certainly explains you—but you're acting like any master vampire needs to be brought down like a rabid dog. Most vamps are real pieces of work sure, but here's no reason to think all master vamps are like the one who killed— The one who turned you."

"The DSA—"

"The DSA knows about this?"

"The DSA has *protocols* for it. They know about Tommy now, and they know it—he—can happen again."

"So, what will happen if they think there's one in New Orleans?"

I sighed.

"I'm here to *tell* them if there's one in New Orleans; they didn't just send me down here to help keep stupid teenagers from donating. If they think there's even a *chance*, they'll round up every vamp for testing—and any vamp that can breed... well, how they deal with him will depend on how 'reliable' he is. Best case, indefinite quarantine as a lethal disease vector."

"That's not right, *chèr*. The government can't—"

"The government can and it *should*. Look." I pinched

the bridge of my nose, searched for words.

"Paul, vamps are parasites. Last night I committed felony assault *three times* to feed, and it doesn't matter that it didn't hurt and none of my donors remember it. You *know* that. My legal alternative, what I've done since I got here, is voluntary donors. But what am I doing then? Feeding a junkie's habit, that's what I'm doing! I'm a freaking drug pusher."

"You get some of them out—"

"Yeah, and so *what*? Every vamp in this town supports at least three fang addicts—a lot more if we're greedy. They pay us *real* well, Paul, directly or not, and get vamped so often that they end up half-enthralled, completely susceptible to any vamp's influence. It's why you don't like us any more than I do. The only reason we're not a new addiction epidemic is we can't *breed* so there's only so many of us to go around. Can you imagine if there were hundreds of us? Thousands?"

I gave him a chance to say something. Anything. He didn't.

"And then there's the wannabe-vamps, like Acacia. How many do you think there are who're willing to pay big to trade their suntans for eternal youth and the freaking coolness of it all if it's a sure bet? You don't need a psychotic murdering rapist like Tommy. Say you've got a 'sane' master vamp—they'd be lining up to pay big bucks to get turned and all you'd need is one master vamp progeny going batshit for us to be dancing the Apocalypse Waltz. And how many crime lords—or governments for that matter—would pay or force a master vamp to vampirize their muscle? How 'bout an insane regime like North Korea used to be, with an all-supervamp special force? Talk about *bioterrorism*. Do you think normal people are going to tolerate the threat as our numbers grow?"

"Jacky, *chèr*."

I stopped, looked around. The praying parishioner had gone—hopefully we hadn't chased him away.

I forced my voice lower. "It's not inevitable, really. Maybe one in thirty vamps can create progeny, but since that's a deep, deep, government secret, how would a potential master vamp find out he was one? Everybody knows that vampires can't reproduce except on that one-in-a-thousand chance, and most of us aren't stupid or crazy enough to try and turn someone when it will probably kill them. But the one who's tried, and had it work? Like Acacia's or Leroy's hypothetical sire? If it worked once he'll try it again. When it works again, he'll *know*. And then unless we get him, unless *I* take him down or take him in, one way or another we're climbing into that hand basket for our quick ride to Hell."

Paul's face had gone hard, his mouth tight, but he shook his head.

"We've got an audience," he said, pointing with his chin. Carefully glancing back, I saw a tall dark-haired man talking to a priest—both just as carefully not looking at us. Paul surprised me.

"Kiss me," he whispered.

I blinked. *Huh?*

"Give me a long goodbye, and *go.*"

Aha. I stood, then bent down to hold his face for a long kiss. Able to see past his ear, I watched our audience look away. "Emerson had to let Acacia's brother go," Paul whispered as we separated.

"Wait, what?" My lips felt full of blood. *Focus, girl.*

"Be careful—I'll meet you at the car," he said low enough that I barely heard him. I remembered my cue.

"Goodbye," I said, trying not to overplay and sound like a dramatic heroine in a sob-scene. I turned and walked away without looking back.

I'd scouted St. Louis Cathedral before, and now I took advantage of its best spy-feature: the back way out through St. Anthony's Garden. If the tall dark man was a tail then there was no way he could follow me out past Paul without being hugely obvious, and the chance he'd sent somebody else around was small.

New Orleans had more than its share of "haunted" places, and St. Anthony's Garden was one. In the old days it had been a dueling ground, though its monument was for sailors who died somewhere else. Through its gate, I turned and headed up Royal Street, moving with the happy, swirling Carnival crowd.

Would Paul confront them? Or just play it out and go?

Being unescorted meant I attracted a few calls and offers, so ducking into a Mardi Gras shop, I bought a festival mask and feathered beret. On impulse I also picked up a cheap krewe costume, a satin jacket, bright purple with gold trim and fringing. Changing in the shop, I folded up my leather jacket and stuffed it in a purchase bag, inserted myself into a happy group of masked partiers, and let them sweep me out the door and up the street.

I didn't need to feed, but a cheerfully assertive college boy who introduced himself as Brent bought me a beer-yard of dark Guinness and I was happy to hold onto his arm. I stayed with the party for a couple of blocks, even yelled "Throw me something, mister!" with them when a walking krewe in carnival feathers mamboed by behind a brass band and drum major. I caught two strings of gold and silver beads for my efforts and added them to my costume. At the corner of Royal and Dumaine, I handed Brent the half-full yard with a whisper implying I had to find the lady's room, then ducked into the crowded corner bar and back out through the Dumaine Street door.

Up Dumaine I found an alley that took me away from the street, where I took off the mask, cap, and beads, and traded jackets. I stuffed everything into the bag, hopped three fences on my way through the close warren of buildings, and came out on St. Phillip Street. From there it was only a five minutes' easy walk to the car, but I stood in the shadow of a closed drapery shop and watched it and everyone in sight of it for another ten.

Where was Paul?

My cell buzzed, startling me. It was Paul.

"*Jacky?*"

"Running late?" I asked, putting a smile on my face in case anyone was watching.

"Not exactly. Check the windshield."

I froze, looked around. No one close to me was doing anything other than passing, and there were damn few line-of-sight angles to see me from that didn't involve breaking and entering.

"Paul—"

"I'm okay, just do it."

Stepping out of the shadows, I hurried over to the car. Someone had stuck a business card under the left wiper. It was matte-black, blank except for a silver-engraved razor-thin crescent on one side: the symbol of the Midnight Ball.

"Hello, Ms. Bouchard," a different voice said in my ear. *"Do you have it?"*

I waited until I could control myself. "Yes. If you hurt—"

"Understood. He will be waiting for you when you return." He hung up and I stared at my phone, thoughts fighting for priority. The loudest demanded that I find whoever had Paul, nail him to the wall so he couldn't mist away, and explain his mistake in a reasonable voice while he screamed. He'd heal afterward, but he'd get the point. I put that one off with promises.

No demands, no instructions, but the card only meant one thing: the Master of Ceremonies wanted to see me.

Well, now I wanted to see *him*.

Chapter Thirteen

It is the eve of St. George's Day. Do you not know that tonight, when the clock strikes midnight, all the evil things in the world will have full sway?

Bram Stoker, *Dracula*.

Who waits for midnight?

Jacky Bouchard.

The Midnight Ball might be just a few nights away, but now Lalaurie House was dark, all but one of its windows shuttered behind their fancy ironwork. The house squatted on the corner of Royal Street and Governor Nicholas, three stories of old evil and rumored hauntings even before the Master of Ceremonies bought it and restored it to its old French Creole splendor.

Where else would a rich vamp live, but a home built

by an insanely cruel woman who kept a torture chamber in her attic?

I stepped through the street gate and handed the card to the guard standing in the recessed entryway. He grinned and half-tore it like it was a movie ticket before handing it back and beckoning me through the door. Vessy, the Master of Ceremonies' assistant (advisor, enforcer, right-hand man?) greeted me in the shadowed entry hall. He was a tall, stringy vamp; the guard beside him, impressively muscled with ornamental scars crisscrossing his bald head and bare biceps, easily outweighed him.

Scarhead held out a silver platter large enough to host a small roast pig.

"Weapons, phone," he said. Vessy didn't say anything, but his eyes widened when I dropped the Desert Eagle and oversized knife on the platter, ringing it like a gong. I added my cellphone, held out the bag and smiled at them. Showing fang.

Scarhead looked at Vessy, who shrugged, passing on the body search and leaving me my little Kel-Tec, a comforting weight at the small of my back.

"Take me to your *mathster*," I lisped. Vessy glared but Scarhead barked a laugh, set the platter and bag on a hall table, and led me up the sweeping staircase to the second floor.

I've never been superstitious, and since the nightmares that took place in Lalaurie House happened nearly two hundred years before the Event, I didn't believe the ghosts of tortured and murdered slaves haunted the place seeking revenge. The Master of Ceremonies had had years to make the place his own, but I would have bet a month's Sentinels pay that at least one of the high society vamp's staff was an undercover cop. I doubted he'd buried more bodies under the floor, so that left out any post-Event hauntings.

But Lalaurie House still creeped me out.

Part of it was the low lighting provided by fake electric candles and the soft music piped into every room, sometimes so low it played just on the edge of my hearing. Most of it was the way that all the staff moved silently on soft-soled shoes, without talking or even acknowledging anyone's presence—like they were ghosts themselves, moving in a world where I was invisible. They were performing, and the entire house was a stage. It was creepy as hell, and what did it say about the playwright?

So I didn't look at them, or at Scarhead when he stopped at the top of the stairs; I knew where the library was, and my host would be waiting for me there. It was the best stage in the house. Scarhead had to skip around me to open the library door before I did, then rush to arrive beside me when I kept going to stop on the carpet in the middle of the room.

"Ms. Bouchard, Sir," he said, not near as smoothly as he'd have liked.

"Thank you Richard. That will be all."

He *silently* closed the door behind him as the owner of Lalaurie House turned away from the unshuttered window, the one I'd seen from the street. We studied each other.

I didn't know why he bothered to wear the black Carnival mask that always covered half his face. It didn't hide his dark hair or steel grey eyes or disguise his deep voice, a voice that matched the large and muscled body inside the tailored suits he wore. His crisp bowtie circled a neck I couldn't have gotten both hands around, and heavy rings sat on thick but not stubby fingers. The vamps that attacked me had used masks to hide their identities, but if he danced down the street in full krewe costume in eye-bleeding color, covered in fringe and beads, I'd recognize him from a block away.

The fanciful image tugged at the corners of my mouth, and I let it just to push his buttons. His hands tightened on the head of his cane, and I decided to push some more.

"Nice stick. Does it have a sword in it?"

The jab missed; he chuckled. "Indeed. A necessary accessory for any gentleman. Thank you for coming."

"Bite me."

"Later, perhaps. Would you care to sit? I heard about today's unfortunate event. I assure you that I have had nothing to do with the attempts on your life, but we have much to discuss."

"Let Paul go."

"Paul is also necessary, since my goal is a civil conversation with *Artemis*."

No one can be as *still* as a vampire, and only my eyes moved as I measured him. I could put three bullets in his head, take his sword cane while he was stunned, remove his head and be out the window with it before anyone could stop me. Except the glass looked bulletproof and was covered by ironwork. I could mist—but the outside walls were probably not air permeable and I'd find myself trapped in the house in another fight with vamps that knew the rules better than I did.

Damn it. Trading his head for Paul would have been the surest bet.

"If anything happens to Paul," I said, "I'd better be ashes in the wind or I will burn this freaking Disney mansion to the ground."

"I believe you. Now that we have each established that we are too dangerous to be trifled with, may we move on?"

"May I call you MC? Because Master of Ceremonies is just way too formal. What does your mother call you?"

"Ms. Bouchard—"

"MC it is."

"Ms. Bouchard."

"And can I be honest? The raven in the corner is just one prop too many. Really. Because it's not at all, you know, *creepy.*"

"Ms. Bouchard!"

"I can do this all night, MC. Since you want to *talk,* I mean."

He sank into one of the room's high-backed chairs and regarded me with a frown.

"I don't think you appreciate the—"

"You know, you really need a white cat to stroke." I relaxed into the chair opposite him. "Since you haven't dragged me up to the attic, you grabbed Paul because you want something. Since I'm not cooperating until Paul is free and that window behind you is open, there's no need for me to listen to you till then, is there? So what have you got to drink? 'Cause I feel like an A positive. I'm guessing your coffee is bayou mud."

The clock in the corner (Marc the Raven's perch) ticked while I tried to recognize the strain of orchestra music teasing my ears. MC's mouth finally smoothed out, and he reached into his jacket to withdraw his cellphone. I *didn't* tense, ready to pull the Kel-Tec and do my best if I didn't like what I heard. Instead, he gave instructions that Paul was to be released and given the phone. More time ticked by until he nodded and tossed the cell to me.

"*Jacky? Where are you?*"

MC rose and opened the window. "I'm fine," I said, watching him. "Did they hurt you?"

"*They suckered me.*" Paul sounded disgusted. "*But I'm good.*"

"Where?"

"*Jackson Square.*" I could hear the jazz band behind him. No, he wouldn't want to pull his piece or go all beastly there.

"You're walking away. Lose them and call again when you're safe." I handed the phone back to MC, who gave more instructions and then called for drinks. Scarhead came back with an opened bottle of wine and a glass,

another bottle and a beer glass for me. I raised my
eyebrows: Blue Moon. We poured for ourselves and
waited in silence. I didn't want to be impressed, but I was;
not many people could stand silence, especially in
"delicate negotiations."

When the phone rang again MC answered it
unhurriedly, then handed it to me.

"*I'm back in the precinct*," Paul said tersely. "*Now
where are you?*"

"I'm having a friendly conversation with our Master of
Ceremonies. He's expressing his concerns. I'll call for a
pickup."

Paul swore. "*Half an hour, Jacky. Then I'm coming in
with every gun available.*"

"That's sweet. I'll be good." I was certain I heard a
chuckle from MC as I hung up, but he accepted the phone
with a serious face.

"I suppose our sting operation is blown?" I asked.
He shook his head.

"I quite approve of it. Continue, by all means."

"Well hell, more crinoline."

That got a louder chuckle and he waved at the goth
themed room around us. "We all make sacrifices. Now,
may I speak with Artemis?"

"I left her in Chicago. What do you know about her?"

"I know that Marie Bouchard had a daughter named
Eleanor, who left New Orleans thirty years ago. I know
that she and her husband, Fred Siggler were killed in an
'animal attack' in Chicago five years ago when their

daughter Jacqueline was abducted—shortly before a nightstalking urban myth named Artemis became active. I know she went public and joined the Sentinels last fall, but disappeared again early this year. And now a young vampire named Jacqueline Bouchard is living with her grandmother."

"I never went public as a vampire."

"No, but a black clad, hooded vigilante superhero, only ever seen at night, who is inhumanly strong and possesses some kind of 'teleportation' power...well. How did you feed?"

"Gangstas and players, mostly. I'm not a superhero. I can pass for one if you squint, and God knows my best friend thinks I'm one."

"I'm glad to hear it, and now I'd like Artemis to work for me."

I put down my glass, careful not to tighten up. "No."

"I'm sorry to hear that."

"Like I give a rat's ass. Look MC, obviously I've read things all wrong and am too dumb to live. I should have known this town would have a vampire mafia—you're practically *famiglia*, the way everyone talks about you, and Sable almost kisses your ring. So, no." I could feel my blood rising, firing my nerves. Three shots, and the window was open with nobody else close enough to stop me from misting away.

He sipped his wine, eyes not leaving mine.

"I prefer to think of us as a mutual aid society. And if our interests march together?"

"Oh, well then that's just fine. Like my friends in Chicago won't mind my crawling in bed with the mob if there's *something in it for me*. Screw you and the pale horse you rode in on."

He shrugged. "I posted bail on Acacia's brother and cousins."

"*Why?*"

"Family is a wonderful thing. Should the boys be punished for picking the wrong target?"

"They put a stake in me! How did you..."

"Darren works for me, or rather for the LH Association and so for the vampire community. You'd be amazed how many people try to claim assault or even date rape after an evening with a vampire; a good lawyer on retainer is a must."

"Yeah, like *influencing* anyone you want into wanting to give it up for you shouldn't be, you know, *discouraged*."

His eyes hooded. "Believe me Ms. Bouchard, it is. There is a reason why vampires in my town only openly feed in certain well known places. But we are wandering from the point, which is that I have been informed what happened, or you suspect happened, to Acacia. The police have questioned her and discounted her brother's testimony, but however she turned, if she truly didn't recognize her kin then she has been enthralled. I want you to take care of it."

I opened my mouth, closed it. "By 'take care of' you mean..."

He beat his cane against the floor. "I want her *free*.

And when you find the one who enthralled her, I do not want to hear about it on CNN. I do not want to hear about it *at all*. I want him delivered to me. I am a peaceful man, Ms. Bouchard, by which I mean I like things peaceful and will do what is necessary to preserve that state. Leroy is too visible and is already engaged in looking into other matters, so I want Artemis to do what she does so well."

He sat back. "You may consult with Leroy. You will not involve the police in your investigation. Do we understand each other?"

The *or else* hung unstated between us. I picked up and finished my Blue Moon. "And *my* price?"

"Yes?"

"If you know what I am, then you understand Leroy is like me."

He nodded.

"I want his sire."

"Done," he said and I blinked. *Too easy*. I hid my confusion. There'd be time to think about it later.

"Are we finished, then?"

Now he smiled, and I blinked again. It was an open smile, stuffed full of silent laughter. "Surely you'd best be off, before your partner storms the villain's lair."

A partner I'd just been told not to involve in any "solution" by New Orleans' vampire godfather. Well, hell.

Chapter Fourteen

The Department of Superhuman Affairs is misunderstood; they aren't the Men In Black. Mostly they're a research and information department, and they coordinate operations with teams in the FBI, Secret Service, and US Marshals' Office. Although they can invoke emergency powers, they have to work within the framework of federal law—which is why they also use relatively autonomous civilian assets like me. I was the left hand the right hand didn't want to know about.

Jacky Bouchard, *The Artemis Files.*

My to-do list was getting longer: find out who paid for the hitter who almost got Grams and bury them; find out if someone had turned Acacia and deal with them; find out who had turned Leroy and do same. In my nearly five years as Artemis I'd never *killed* anybody other than my sire. Now time was getting short and my Shovel List was up to three deep—except you didn't bury them in this town. It might be a list of *one* if some criminal mastermind was behind it all, but that only happened in movies.

One or many, I needed to get some idea of who the enemy was before the Midnight Ball.

By the time Paul pulled up in the Cadi I was mentally subdividing my lists. Looking purely disgusted with himself, he told me all about how they'd caught up with him right outside the cathedral. He didn't know who "they" were, but the public grab had involved at least five—three as cover while only two held guns on him—and they hadn't even tried to take him anywhere; just the threat of deadly violence in the middle of the crowds had been enough. They'd found some tables and drunk some beers until I'd insisted they let him walk.

He was still burning over it. And he was going to be a problem.

I wasn't a team player. After nearly five years solo, a few months working with the Sentinels and then a few weeks with Paul hadn't changed my habits. And if Artemis was going to go to war then I had to distance my activities from Paul—I didn't need the Master of Ceremonies to tell me that. He might be able to go all furry, but he was still way too mortal and he carried a badge; getting him out of the way until I'd buried my enemies was by far the safest way.

To my surprise, I didn't want to.

I missed Hope terribly—missed having someone at my back, even if having a BFF who believed I was better than I was had been a pain. Not to mention having the assets of a team nobody in their right mind would mess with... Paul finished the story of his night before I thought to ask where we were going, and when I did he finally smiled. Grinned like a kid with a surprise to share.

"We're almost there," he said, turning the corner from Marketplace to Barracks Street. *Almost there* actually meant not too many blocks from where we started, but he'd driven roundabout to spot any tails. The Old US Mint sat on our right, a solid business row on our left—one long wall of closed-up shops, ugly, patchy grey walls and black-shuttered doors exposed by the light of iron streetlamps. Probably someone had bought the entire street of joined buildings to redevelop it, then couldn't make it in the current economic crunch. Now locals used them to post concert ads and sale signs.

Paul turned left onto Decatur, hit a switch, and a garage door tucked in the back of the old building's corner shuddered open. Pulling us into the space, he turned off the car as the door closed behind us. The one bare bulb illuminating the space had come on automatically, revealing a dusty car space and empty boxes. We weren't all that far from Grams'—or from Lalaurie House, but everything in the Quarter was close by Chicago standards.

"What is this?" I asked as we got out.

"I know you can find your own place for the daytime," Paul said, handing me a flashlight and taking us through a door and into the shop's old storage space. "But you really need a safe house. I'd been going to show you this but you dragged me off to church." He opened the storage room door.

"Three years ago, this place got occupied by a local gang and they forted it up. Take a look." He waved theatrically, shining his own light on the shuttered windows. They were barred behind the shutters. I rapped an interior wall: reinforced—steel plate? Or they could have filled the hollow space with old phone books. Maybe both.

"Upstairs is the same, and we're talking steel shutters with fire-holes and serious locks. The garage has a back way out, and worst case scenario they could get out over the roofs. They worked for the cartels, shipped hundreds of kilos of Coke through here—more worried about rival gangs than the cops."

The air smelled dead, trapped, and dust motes danced in the flashlight beams as our steps kicked up the dandruff of at least a year.

"What happened?"

"We happened. Rolled them up in one big operation last year, and this wasn't the only place we seized. The Cadi was part of the lot. But here's the payoff." He took me back into the storage room, flicked the light on. Grabbing a shelf, he pulled the back wall open to expose a steel door.

"St. Augustine made me think of it," he said, unlocking it. "They kept all the drugs back here in the vault—which doubled as a security room." The room was empty except for a half-assembled motorcycle engine, a box of parts, and a can of motor oil. Somebody's hobby? He showed me a circuit box on the wall; opened, it was a Christmas tree of lights and small screens.

"They wired the place for serious security; every door and window is wired in, there are cameras you can monitor from here. And best of all—" he tapped what looked like a hatch with his foot. "This goes right into the sewers, with an opening big enough that they could dump the room's contents in minutes. It's the perfect escape route for you if anyone comes after you here."

He turned and looked at me. "Well, *chèr*? I got Emerson's permission, got the power and water turned back on this afternoon. It's a dump, but it's as safe as anywhere in town. Got the car from impound on the same deal. Less visible than the van. I made sure the trunk is sealed against light and drilled a few holes in the bottom for you; you can use it as an emergency shelter if we get you caught out in the day."

"I—" I didn't know what to say. He hated vampires, didn't like voodoo even if he wore a gris-gris pouch, only tolerated working with a bloodsucker as a necessary part of his job. So, *why*?

"Emerson told me the review of Acacia's blood warrants came back negative," he said. "We can't link her to another vamp. Questioning Leroy about the attack was a dead end—the descriptions he gave us led nowhere, which means we've got vamps in town that aren't on the radar."

He ran fingers through his hair, face full of concern. "*Chèr,* we don't know who *they* are, or why they're coming at us."

I pulled my thoughts together.

"We're done, Paul. At least for now."

"What?"

"They're coming after *me.* Not you, and Grams was just in the way. We're not going out fishing together while I'm a target, I'm no use to Emerson's V-Juice investigation, even as a material witness, and I wouldn't accept protective custody if he offered it. So I'm not your job anymore."

"*Chèr—*"

"Who else knows about this place?"

"Nobody who knows about us, but—"

"So it should be fine. Thank Emerson for me, but besides keeping my head down, what do you think I'm supposed to be doing? Nothing the police can know anything about, and that means you. Unless you're willing to get dirty?"

I shut up and watched him connect the dots back to my DSA job, kept my face neutral as his mouth twisted like he'd tasted something foul. Cops *hated* classified government ops. If he blamed a distant federal agency that was fine with me—no reason for him to know I wasn't involving them either.

"So you've got, what?" he asked, putting a nasty twist on it. "A license to *kill*?"

"Something like that." *Nothing* like that, but if I wanted him to step away then he had to see me as an unfriendly agent, not a partner to protect.

He turned away, shoulders hunched, and punched the wall. "Shit, Jacky."

"It was fun," I said to his back. "We should do it again, sometime."

"Are you going to stick around after it's over?"

A shrug. "Family's here." That much was true. I stayed where I was, but when he made to go I couldn't leave it at that. "Paul?"

He turned around. "What?"

"I— You know why I'm different from your average bloodsucker. What about you? Why not a... *loup-garou*? You said it was family, so what happened?"

"What happened?" He laughed, not a happy sound. "You remember my momma's family is Italian?"

"Yeah."

"Momma thought I should know my roots, sent me to Italy to stay with my uncles every summer." He put his back to the wall, slid down to sit on the floor. "So my third trip there, my uncles took me and my other male cousins into the hills on the Feast of St. John—that's the summer solstice. They've got a huge open cave, and they built a bonfire and told us about God's Hounds, the *Benandanti*— the Good Walkers. We drank the family wine, they put on wolf skins, sang, danced around, and invited me to join."

He closed his eyes. "Lord, was I drunk, and I think there was something else in it. I could barely see straight, my heart felt like it was going to explode... Next thing, I wasn't wearing a wolf, I *was* one. Really impressed them, me; according to the family story, they went wolfing in the dream, fought evil in the spirit world—only time a *Benandante* wolfed in his own body, serious evil was brewing he'd been chosen specially to fight."

"So the family tradition shaped your breakthrough. Do you...go all furry often?"

"Hardly. The other night was the first time in a fight. But I'm damn tough and quick, hard to influence, which is why I got assigned to Emerson's team. Some nights I go camping on private land, but I never lose control and slaughter horny teens."

"Good to know. So have you found the serious evil you're supposed to fight?"

He looked at me, eyes cold. "Pretty much this whole town, *chèr*. One more thing—I found Leroy. Competition fencing world is a small one, spent the day looking at team pictures of national leagues, me. He's Canadian, from a little town outside Montreal. Don't know yet why a *Québécois* is imitating a Frenchman. Be careful."

He got out without many more words, leaving the car keys in exchange for a promise from me that I'd call if I needed him. He promised to fix Gram's security situation; I didn't know much about post-Event magic, but, even if Grams had the real mojo, how reliable could it be? I couldn't count on every hitter who went after Grams getting terminally clumsy.

I listened until I heard the garage door close. Would

he call a cab? I realized I didn't know where he lived; was it in the Quarter? Dragging one of the steel shelves from the storeroom back into the security room, I lay out and inventoried my gear, trying not to think about it. Alone was how I worked, and Paul was a big boy.

And however willing Paul was, I couldn't make him part of what I was going to have to do. As strangely nice as he was being, there was no way he would help me pull off an abduction right under Detective Emerson's nose.

Chapter Fifteen

I laugh in the face of danger. Laugh my ass off, usually. A good fight lets me work out my issues.

Jacky Bouchard, *The Artemis Files.*

I needed a supplier. Big Brother wasn't *always* watching but he could always listen, so I'd made sure my emergency kit included a burner phone. As Artemis, they were all I'd ever used, and since I needed the information anyway... I placed a phone call to Leroy for some clarification, an address, and Darren's number. MC had given permission after all, and even if I couldn't trust him or Leroy with my safety there were some things I desperately needed.

When I called Darren to give him the list and find out what happened to Acacia's kinfolk after he bailed them out, I half expected to hear they'd "disappeared." Instead he gave me the address of a cheap hotel in the Warehouse District; one of them was still in traction at Tulane University Hospital and the other three weren't leaving town until he was out. Cheerful as before, Darren was happy to do some shopping for me with an arranged drop. Something wasn't right with that boy; how could a lawyer *smile* all the time? I could hear his shit-eating grin over the phone.

Making Masson Guns and Ammo my first stop, I picked up my first modified Desert Eagle and gave Bobby a few more anti-vampire tips to calm him down. The man was seriously thinking about getting his family out of town. Firing two boxes of rounds downrange to get the feel, I decided Bobby didn't charge enough; the grip fit like an extension of my hand. The big gun felt awkward in its new shoulder-holster, but the heavy knife and spare clips counterbalanced it a bit. Most important, nothing looked too obvious under my leather jacket; just a little influence would keep people from noticing. After making sure Bobby knew how much I appreciated his work (really, the man was an artist), I headed out again.

Back in Chicago, I'd learned to never make a move unless I knew the ground, knew who I was dealing with. *I'd* picked the fights and the battlefield. Here I was the hunted, didn't know the hunter, and didn't know what he knew. Which meant, even ignoring a looming DSA decision, I couldn't wait, *had* to push, *had* to find him before he found me. To do that I had to pull on the only string I had—and it was attached to a serious police investigation.

I was going to need help. Fortunately I knew where to find it.

The Hearst Hotel had seen better days. In fact *any* day must have been better—it had the look of a property where the owner had stopped paying for maintenance and was milking it for what he could get before the place got condemned; most of its business was probably hourly now, but even the hookers and their clients disappeared by witching hour.

Simple was best, and I'd planned on getting Dupree's room number from the night desk guy, then knocking. Except that someone beat me to it; nobody answered when I rang the bell on the counter. The cage closing off the counter didn't let me lean over, but standing higher and looking down, I saw a shoe on the floor, twisted in the overturned chair. Smelling blood, I was suddenly glad I'd fed last night. *Oh shit.*

Going still and listening didn't tell me anything. Finally risking the mist, I passed through the cage grill.

Shit shit *shit!* Dead night-guy lay on the floor, throat ripped out, still warm, not nearly enough blood outside of him. I turned to the counter, found Dupree's information and room number already up on the screen, grabbed the desk phone and dialed 9-1-1.

"Calling for Detective Emerson, French Quarter Precinct!" I shouted as soon as a cool, professional voice answered. "Vampire homicide, desk clerk at the Hearst Hotel, unknown vamps still present!"

"What is your—" I hung up, checked the back office, misted back through the grill and raced for the stairs.

Jumping into an unknown situation sucked, but if I

had to do it the best way was to jump in fast and hard. If they didn't see me coming, at least I'd have achieved mutual confusion. I passed one messy drunk on the way to the third floor but no more bodies, a good sign, and heard the first shots before I hit the third floor landing. I went *through* the door into the hallway, Desert Eagle in one hand and Arkansas toothpick in the other.

The black-hooded vamps standing in the hall turned my way as the shattered door hit the opposite wall: two of them, teeth red, with familiar machetes.

Looking for me and just got here early? I laughed, blood rising. *My turn.*

Loadouts of frangible rounds meant I didn't have to worry about missing my targets, blowing through a wall and killing someone I wasn't trying to, and I dialed in while they were still reacting to my entrance. *Boom boom, boom boom!*

Contrary to the movies, bullets don't throw people around. I walked the shots from Target One's chest up to his neck and head as thunder slammed the air of the close hallway. His head flopped grotesquely as he staggered, dropped his machete, went to mist and faded. Target Two made it to mist before I serviced him more than twice, lasersight leading my shots, and he attacked. Feeling him swirl past me, I laughed as I swept into mist and *pushed.*

I'd had plenty of time to think about the rooftop fight and figure out what had happened. Riding the mist felt like running on a tightrope—balanced, in motion, never quite falling—and a hard jab of influence could push me right off that rope to fall back into flesh like it had repeatedly that night. But two could play and Target Two stumbled in flight as I followed him down, going solid behind him, pistol to the base of his skull before he could recover.

Boom.

The shot half-decapitated him, and I finished the job with a backswing slice of the thirteen-inch knife. Target One was nowhere, and there were no other shots. With only one round left in the magazine and one in the chamber, I swapped in a reload as I moved sideways down the hallway, back to the wall.

"Hello?" I called, keeping my gun up as I closed on the open hotel room door. They might not be able to hear me; gunfire in close quarters hammered living ears pretty badly. For a moment I thought *my* hearing had been impaired, then realized I was hearing sirens.

"Hello?" I called again. "The police are on their way."

"Who is that?" someone shouted from the room.

"Are you all right?" I tried.

"Rick's—God, he's dead! He's—"

"Shut up!" A different, steady voice. "Ma'am, I don't want to be rude, but you should stay away." Even half-yelling, he had the same soft Cajun accent as Paul and Acacia.

"Why?" I called back. "This is where the *fun* is. You bayou-boys have already met me, so I'll just stay right here until the cops arrive." *Gee, coming on too strong?* I forced my voice lower. "Mr. Dupree?"

Someone in the room sobbed, choked it off.

"Miss Bouchard?" Mister Steady Voice said carefully. "Were you the one shooting out there?"

"Yep. The police will be coming up the stairs in a few minutes, and we have to talk."

"*Don't go out there—*" A slap, heavy and backhanded, cut the screamer off and a piece of me winced; someone wasn't having a good night. He was going to need serious therapy. And drugs. I could have used some...

"Miss Bouchard?" Dupree called. "I'm coming out."

I holstered the gun and dropped the knife, checked myself for blood, and tried to look harmless. Well, less scary. I'd come to ask for help, and that hadn't changed.

Robert Dupree was a bigger, harder version of his sister and I recognized him as the guy who'd put a stake in me three nights ago. He looked down at the body, at the head bumped up against the wall trim and leaking blood into the carpet. The guy's mask had managed to stay on, but it couldn't make him look any better.

"Jesus."

"He'll get better," I said.

"Rick won't."

"I don't suppose he will. The police will be coming up the stairs soon, Mr. Dupree, and I need to ask you a question."

"Owe you that, I guess," he said roughly.

Oh, you think? I kept that inside-voice, putting influence behind my words. "Are you *certain* that Acacia didn't recognize you? The police didn't believe your story."

He shook his head, looking sick. "They told me about

the V-Juice, Ma'am, and when they interviewed Steph themselves she knew who she was, recognized my picture. But Ma'am? When I found her at Angels the first night, she had no idea who I was—tried to *come on* to me!"

That'll do. "Then I can help you, Mr. Dupree. What's your cell number?" He didn't know what to think, but gave it anyway while I punched it into my burner-phone's memory. Shouts echoed up the stairwell and I hesitated; time to go, but...

Sloppy crying leaked from the open hotel room. Dammit, I couldn't *be* here!

"Dupree? Your boy in there is in for a lifetime of screaming nightmares and alcoholic self-medication. I can take it away—make sure what happened never gets written into his long-term memory."

"You can *do* that?"

A shrug. "He'll be useless as a witness, but, yeah, if you can buy me a couple of minutes."

He hesitated only a second, nodded, and stood aside.

There were nights when I wanted to stake them all.

The small hotel room dripped red and I ignored the heady, copper reek. Rick, the obvious corpse, sprawled facedown by the bed. It looked like someone had ripped his throat out and splattered it on the walls before throwing him across the room. There'd been no drinking here; all Rick's blood was present and accounted for. My reason for staying crouched in the corner, the gun in his hands shaking so badly if he managed to fire it he'd probably shoot himself in the head. That might be his plan, and I didn't want to care.

He'd held one of my arms while Dupree staked me.

"Don't!" he shrieked when I stepped over Rick. Damn it, he'd probably shoot *Dupree* if I didn't get the gun away from him.

"You're going to be fine…"

"Marco," Dupree supplied.

"You're going to be fine, Marco," I whispered, gently extending my influence. "You're tired, this is a bad dream, if you close your eyes you'll wake up and know everything's okay…" I kept talking, moving closer as his shuddering breath smoothed, his frantic blinking slowed, and the gun lowered. Behind me, Dupree closed the door. Good; with no open door and no noise in here, the body in the hall would focus the responders' attention for at least a few minutes.

The words gave Marco something to hang on to as my influence washed over him. His eyes fluttered, closed, his grip relaxed and I caught the gun, held it behind me for Dupree to take, lifted his wrist. His hand flopped, boneless.

I looked back. "I'm going to have to…"

"Do it," Dupree said. "Can't do him worse."

Not true but I didn't say it. Kneeling, I pulled his shirtsleeve down to expose the suicide vein. A gentle bite, barely a touch, blood flowed and Marco was mine.

I drank shallowly, aware of Dupree behind me, and ended at thirty. Lifting my head to meet Marco's open and dilated eyes, I moved up and gently kissed his forehead. "Forget, Marco," I whispered, my breath stirring his damp hair as I poured all my blood-infused influence into him. "Forget your fear, forget the fight, forget the hours of tonight."

I'd thought he couldn't get any looser but he melted, eyes closing again. I pushed him deeper into sleep, then picked him up and lay him on the bed as the police pounded on the hotel room door.

Dupree stared, eyes wide, like he was seeing...what? "Your eyes," he said.

What? Reaching up, I realized my cheeks were wet. Why? I wiped while he shouted out the door, then carefully opened it.

Two helmeted cops wearing flack-jackets with silver crosses made of duct tape across their chests burst into the room, Kriss Super-V autos ready. They stared at me, at Rick, and almost started shooting. I stayed *still*, not at all interested in finding out what kind of rounds those guns fired. When Emerson stepped in behind them I didn't know whether to sigh or swear.

The night was just never going to end.

Chapter Sixteen

Faeces evinio. Shit happens. So true I had it tattooed, but I've always preferred to be the shit that happens.

Jacky Bouchard, *The Artemis Files.*

I was getting too used to interrogation rooms.

Contrary to older stories, vampires can see themselves in mirrors just fine—at least I hadn't met one who couldn't, which was a good thing considering how vain we all were.

I used the room's one-way mirror to retie my hair; a bunch of it had half escaped its tail sometime tonight. I'd been two nights now without a proper shower so it was a good thing that, being dead, I didn't get oily or flaky skin or otherwise have to worry about body odor, but I was getting a bit dirty here and there and I smelled someone's blood on me somewhere.

Putting my hands down I smiled for the benefit of

whomever was watching, just to bug them. Someone had turned the air-conditioning off, but they could fry an egg on the table and I wouldn't care.

The door opened and Emerson half stepped in, then stopped. "What is this crap?" he yelled behind him. Someone muttered something defensive, and the A/C kicked back on.

He closed the door behind him, loosened his collar, and eyed my manacles; they'd attached my handcuffs to the table by a long chain. I agreed with that bit; since the room wasn't airtight the only way to keep me there was to lock me to something solid and big enough I couldn't take it into mist with me.

"Would you like to take your jacket off?" he asked sarcastically, rolling his eyes at the mirror.

"I'm good."

He laughed sharply. "Hardly. What am I going to tell your grandmother?"

"How are Dupree and Marco?" Emerson had had me cuffed and hustled out of there before some trigger-happy officer shot me.

"*Marco*," he said, "hasn't woken up to tell us. Would you mind telling me why?"

"He's narcoleptic?"

"Jacky..."

"I went to the hotel to *talk*, Emerson. I wanted to make sure they weren't planning on hunting me again. The other vamps got there first—but you were expecting *someone*, weren't you? 'Cause you had to be *on top of the freaking hotel.* You were in the lobby what, a minute after my call? It looks like live bait is your style after all."

"Jacky—"

"I went to *talk*, found the night clerk, made the call, then rendered assistance—which I can do as a private citizen. If you want more, talk to my lawyer—Darren, I'm sure you've met—or cut me loose."

I leaned back, closed my eyes. "Sun's up soon. You really going to waste time with me when you could be interrogating Mister Headless Hood?"

He didn't react to my suggestion, which meant he already knew how impermanent decapitation was for vamps. Damn it, I was the only one who'd been operating without an instruction manual.

When he didn't say anything I opened my eyes. He sat patiently, hands folded on the table, armpits getting dark.

"Are you done?"

"Depends. Give me a phone or a key."

He looked like he'd bitten into something foul. Bringing in Darren, helpful, *hot* Darren, the world's happiest mob lawyer, obviously didn't appeal. I didn't want Darren here either, but Emerson didn't know that.

"Why wasn't Paul in this one?" I pushed.

"He's off the bloodsucker beat. You'll cooperate?"

"I'll tell you everything I know about tonight."

"Sergeant," he raised his voice. One of the cross-wearing officers opened the door. I watched Emerson watch me as the officer produced a key and opened the cuffs, unlocked the table-chain, and left with the clinking armful.

"The night clerk was drained," I said as soon as the door closed. "And not the usual neat way—more like an animal attack. We're talking sicko here, even for a vamp." I didn't ask him if there'd been other attacks like that; if there had been, he wouldn't tell me. "Good luck keeping a mad vampire attack quiet."

"The hotel will cooperate. So much goes on there we could shut them down with a single warrant. Go on."

"I made the call and headed upstairs—"

The interrogation room door opened again, the same officer standing aside to let Darren step in. He nodded to Emerson, smiled at me.

"Don't say anything more, Jacky."

Emerson looked ready to explode.

"Ms. Bouchard is *not* your client, counselor!" So he hadn't believed me.

Darren winked at me. "On the contrary, Lieutenant, we have a professional relationship. I'm sure she would have called as soon as you let her have a phone."

Emerson turned to me, eyes hard. I shrugged helplessly, and Darren helped himself to the metal chair beside me.

"Is my client being charged with anything, Lieutenant?"

Emerson gave him a *look*. "She is helping us with our inquiries," he ground out.

"Jacky?"

I smiled at Darren just to bug Emerson. "He needs to

know what happened."

"Okey dokey." He pulled out a digital voice recorder, turned it on. "If I say *stop*, you'll listen?" I nodded and he turned to Emerson. "Please continue, Lieutenant."

Emerson gave up on the glare, turned back to me. "You headed upstairs. How did you know which room?"

"From the office computer. Someone started shooting before I got there, and there were two vamps in the hall. I didn't see whoever killed the clerk."

"How do you know?"

"Neither of them was covered in blood."

"Okay. Then?"

"I started shooting."

"Rather intemperate, don't you think? Who were they?"

"I don't know."

"Did they have guns? You couldn't have said 'Stop or I'll shoot?' I only want to know why you jumped from seeing two vampires to Game On." Darren held up a finger, looked at me while I thought about it.

Crap. I didn't want Emerson thinking there was some kind of Vampire War going on—especially since there was.

"They were attacking Mr. Dupree," I said finally.

"Did you *see* them fighting?"

"No."

"And you don't know them."

"Objection, Lieutenant," Darren said. "Asked and answered."

"So you started shooting. Then?"

"I got one bad enough that he bugged out. The other one tried for me; I stopped him."

Emerson smiled for the first time, not a pretty smile but an honest one. "And thank you for that. It's damn hard to arrest a resisting vampire without peeling him out of his crypt—if we can find it."

I didn't bother asking if they knew how to *keep* a vamp. So he owed me a favor now, in the unofficial way that policemen could. Hopefully I didn't have to cash it now.

"And then?"

I shrugged. "Not much. Mr. Dupree came out, I stepped inside, I calmed Marco down, and then you guys came through the door."

"You calmed him down."

And there went the favor. Darren looked carefully blank. Emerson could arrest me on assault for feeding from a donor without expressed consent, and though there wasn't a specific *law* against stealing someone's memories, they could fold it into the assault charge too.

"Will he be a reliable witness?" was all Emerson said.

"Mr. Dupree will be more useful."

He drummed his fingers on the table. I *wasn't* asking about the third vamp who'd been in the room when I started shooting. The one who *really* liked blood. Emerson had to have already talked to Dupree so he'd know what to ask me, but he was a cop and cops don't share.

"Dupree's attacker was white, average height. Any ideas?"

Okay, he was sharing now. Not looking at Darren, I reluctantly shook my head. Emerson sighed.

"Sign a statement detailing what you just told me and we'll release your stuff."

"That's it?"

"We've got you on 9-1-1, got Mr. Dupree's testimony, the only thing we can seriously hold you on is Marco—and we're back to no jury ever convicting. I should charge you and lock you up just so you'll stay out of my way, but with your man Darren that would only buy me a day. But Jacky?" He ignored Darren, locking eyes with me in a way people who know us just won't do with a vamp.

"Hmm?"

"Stay out of my way."

I got back to the safe house as blue sky began switching off the stars.

Darren had confirmed my shopping list—with a few hints that knowing what it was for would be helpful. I'd shut him down, hinting back that the less he knew the less he'd have to lie about, and left him outside the precinct. I was beginning to think that the best idea might be to just call in the DSA and let them do what they did best: flood the ground with agents, detain, question, test everybody in sight, and sweep up the mess.

Punching in the security code, I let the system know I was supposed to be here and did a quick review of all monitor alerts. Nobody had been here since I locked it down. I locked myself in, still chewing on the problem.

The problem was the DSA couldn't do all that *quietly*.

As much as I disliked my kind on general principle, Paul was right—few of them deserved the public shit storm a full DSA containment operation would bring. And the public hysteria aside, like I'd told Paul, the fact that *vampires* didn't know about the whole potential master vampire thing was one of the best protections against one discovering what he was.

Which meant I had to get ahead of Emerson's investigation fast—hard to do when I didn't know where it was going. If Emerson managed to roll the vamp they had in custody he might get a lot more than he was looking for. Why had they gone after Dupree? None of it made any sense. On the off-chance, I pulled out my epad and looked at the report pictures on the overdose victims Paul had sent me eons ago. I didn't recognize them, from Angels or anywhere else.

I did a walk-through of the building, even the upstairs, before going back to the security room and resetting the alarms.

There were three possibilities: Dupree knew something dangerous, he might *do* something dangerous, or killing him was a message. But he'd already talked to the police, now that he was a known threat he couldn't be much of one, and *what* message? That the hypothetical master vamp was crazy? At least Emerson had ruled out two suspects; he would have recognized either Leroy or MC from Dupree's description, even under a hood and Mardi Gras mask.

I unrolled my blanket and lay back. There was still only

one string I could see to pull on, and it would be dangerous as hell. My reason for seeking out Dupree hadn't changed; I'd need—

I finally realized what I was looking at. Sometime between when Paul had shown me the place and I'd got back, somebody had written *GET OUT* on the security room wall. With a shaky hand, using... motor oil?

"Seriously? *Seriously?*"

I called Darren on my burner phone and left a message adding two more items to my shopping list, used my cell to text a request to Paul asking who had died in my "safe house" then went to sleep.

The Lone Ranger woke me just before sunset.

Chapter Seventeen

Abduction is such an ugly word; I prefer "forceful relocation."

Jacky Bouchard, *The Artemis Files.*

Casper the Unfriendly Ghost hadn't written anything new on the wall. Paul's answering text told me there were no public records of any recent deaths on the property—but given the previous occupants, anyone who died here probably went into the sewer. I called to check on Grams, said no to coming home.

The next few hours passed tediously. My emergency gear included a bug sweeper and I went over the place inch by inch, even checking the integrity of the security system to make sure Emerson wasn't being clever. I belatedly did the same for the Cadi. Then I haunted the outside, hovering as mist, patiently looking for watchers. Either Emerson trusted me more than I thought or his people were better at surveillance than I was.

Yeah, right.

I called Darren an hour after sunset and gave the drop location—three blocks away behind a closed storefront— and got there on time to watch him arrive and unpack the gear from his car. I waited fifteen minutes after he left before dropping down and tying it all up, and swept it for bugs and transmitters before bringing it home. Then I took my first shower in too many days and got dressed. Overdressed.

Coming back downstairs, I noticed Casper had managed to add an exclamation point and smiled. The exercise was probably good for him, but it would take forever to move beyond the clichés so I unpacked the extras I'd asked for: one toy Ouija board, one digital movie camera, and a tripod. I set both up, leaving the slider in the middle of the board, then packed up the rest of the gear and reset the alarms.

"Okay," I said to the air before turning out the lights. "Express yourself."

A good abduction requires two elements: a successful, *unnoticed* grab, and an untraceable and secure location. The first is important because it buys you time to get to your secure location before interested parties start searching for your victim, the second because again, you don't want to be *found.*

My situation complicated both elements; my target was already a Person of Interest with the police, which made the first element more difficult, and I didn't have time to arrange a location that was both secure and untraceable. If the police started looking and they thought I was involved, they'd find us—which meant I needed for them to be looking away from me long enough for me to get the job done.

For that I needed a specific accomplice and some luck.

Calling Dupree, I asked what his car looked like and told him he'd meet me alone in the parking lot of the Hotel De La Monnaie if he wanted to help his sister. Getting there first, I parked and left the Cadi to roost on the hotel roof.

I didn't trust anyone, but I'd *bet* on family.

And it looked like I'd bet on the right family; Dupree's truck turned into the parking lot twenty minutes later, circled, and stopped in the dark corner near the service entrance. More minutes of watching failed to turn up any tails, no cars stopping for no reason or passengers just sitting. If he still had watchers, they were staying well back, and with his silver tinted windows nobody would see us talk if we kept the cabin light off.

I floated down, alert to the slightest change in the air. Dupree had cracked his windows in the muggy night, I was sitting beside him before he realized—and found myself facing a very big gun.

"Silver loads," he said. "Blessed by the Church."

I watched the gun, not blinking. Damn it—forget about the blessed silver, he'd obviously been learning the lore; he'd know how to finish me. "You thought about last night. Is that a .45?"

"Yep. Tell me why I shouldn't use it."

"Because the police can't help your sister."

"And why can't I?"

"Because however many vamps you kill for good, you can't free her unless you find and kill her master. Maybe not even then."

"And you can?"

"I can try."

"Why?" His aim wavered fractionally; the heavy pistol had to be fatiguing his merely human arm in its cramped position, but that didn't reassure me.

"Honestly? I just want her master." I raised my eyes from the barrel. "And I've been where she is."

"You look it."

I looked down at the black satin, lace-trimmed corset top I wore under my jacket. I had to admire his restraint; most guys would be staring at my chest, or at my legs—so pale they practically glowed in the dark beneath the matching microskirt. His eyes didn't leave my face.

"Ha, ha. Everyone criticizes my wardrobe choices. Do I pick them for me? No. This is what your *sister* wears, you idiot, and I have a wig to match."

"A wig to— What?" *Now* his gun dropped as he tried to figure out what the hell that was supposed to mean. I could try taking it away, or try a little influence, now that he wasn't tight as a wire.

Not a good idea. I'd been his original target, and if he was paranoid enough he might wonder if I was behind last night's attack—my arrival had been awfully convenient. He'd be wondering what kind of game I was running, and if it might be smart to simplify things by burying me.

"Emerson is investigating V-Juice distribution," I said. "He knows Angels is a source and vampires are involved. He's got to be watching Acacia—Stephanie—and he may be right. But even if she's involved she'll never turn on her master unless someone breaks her enthrallment. And Emerson doesn't think vampires can be enthralled."

"Why?"

"Because we can't, not normally, not permanently. But we can if we're enthralled before we're turned, before we become vampires."

A crunch outside the window—Dupree twitched, I flinched, and light played over us as the car that hit the pothole turned at the end of the row and drove by us, exiting the lot. The normal insect-chorus of spring returned and he relaxed. If I'd been alive I'd have broken into a sweat. Dying *hurt*, and this might be the last time.

I should have called Hope.

Dupree's eyes changed and he lowered the gun, released the trigger. Oh good. Nobody was going to die.

He safetied the gun. "Where did you kill?"

"Excuse me?"

"Last night. You've seen death before, bodies. Just now...you're a cold one. You've been on the battlefield."

"So have you."

"Four years Army infantry. Asia, Middle East. You?"

"South Side Chicago, LA. Side of the angels."

He thought about that, nodded. "I'll give you that, after what you did for Marco. Screaming nightmares of your own?"

"Vampires don't dream." *Thank God for that.*

"So, what's the plan?"

Dupree hated the plan, but it had the virtue of flexibility and we could cut out any time up 'til the last step. The best plans let you live to try again.

He left to start his end of it. I stayed to make certain he wasn't followed, then got back in the Cadi. A final call to Father Graff checked another box, and I drove carefully back through the Quarter and into the Garden District.

Darren's information had surprised me; Acacia-Stephanie lived in one of the neighborhood's nicer homes. He'd sent pictures. On a long and narrow property, it had fancy ironwork, a deep front porch with floor to ceiling windows, even a carriage lamp hanging over the front door. Anyone standing on the second floor balcony could look across the street into Lafayette Cemetery, but it was hardly the trendy residence of a punky-goth vamp like "Acacia." Was she living in someone's real estate investment?

Heavy trees cast the streets in deep shadow despite the sliver of moon, and I drove by without stopping or bothering to check for the watchers I assumed to be there.

If they weren't now, they would be.

If Hope had told me two months ago that I'd be dodging cops again, I'd have believed her; as much as I valued her friendship, the Sentinels weren't an easy fit. But stalking other vamps in the Big Easy and trying to do it without leaving a footprint when the cops already knew who I was...

In Chicago, it had been easy to take down gangs that encroached on my "territory"—so many visible moving parts. Even street-level supervillains hadn't been a problem. Half the time I wouldn't even fight them directly; I'd just "question" gang-bangers who never remembered our conversations, get pictures, video, put together a package of information the police could use to get probable cause for warrants, and let the cops and the capes straighten them out. The detectives in my neighborhood precinct had gotten used to finding mysterious envelopes on their desks or car seats (and I almost certainly existed in a thick police file labeled Unknown Informant).

But I'd still had to stay out of sight. As much as people liked us in the movies, in real life vigilantes were considered a Bad Thing by law enforcement. And I didn't know Emerson well enough to know whether *Stay out of my way* meant *Don't let me catch you* or *Stay the hell away from my investigation*. It certainly meant *Mess up my investigation and I'll bury you*.

Even so, this was my element.

I parked on the other side of the block, cracked the window, grabbed my gear, and went to mist. Acacia's driveway was around the corner from the front of her house, with an electric gate. She drove a black motorcycle, a tricked-out Harley nicer than Paul's, and according to Darren she always left just after sunset to join Belladonna at the club. As inseparable as the two of them were in public, I wondered why she lived alone.

I floated, alert, over backyard fences and driveways. TV sounds drifted through open windows, and one neighbor's party spilled onto his back porch, cheerful and loud. A partier might have felt me, a drift of slightly damper air, but no conversations stumbled, nobody shivered and looked around. I found Acacia's driveway and followed it to her darkened backyard.

A few months into my vigilante career, I'd almost gotten seriously hosed in a mission gone bad. I'd been overconfident, screwed up the Breaking and Entering part, and a seriously pissed off pyrokinetic villain had nearly immolated me. After that I found a teacher (the best kind, a Shall Remain Nameless career thief who'd never been caught), and now I perched in a tree across the driveway and looked at Acacia's property with professional eyes and equipment. A system of passive infrared detection and photo-electric beams protected her backyard. When the sensors picked up a heat source (like a human body), the photo-electric system would kick in to "map" the size of the source. Anything smaller than a large dog wouldn't trigger the alarm. Probably.

And it was wrong; the system was worthless against a vamp unless she'd overfed recently and actually had a detectible body temperature. A room-temperature vamp? Forget it. But long minutes of searching failed to turn up anything else. There could be stuff I wouldn't see—but all those systems, like passive magnetic field detectors, would either be just as useless or generate too many false-positives in an outdoor environment to be useful.

I finally repacked everything. Nothing to see here, moving on.

Floating over the property wall and up to the house, I found the kitchen vent and went in. An hour later, I was still wondering what the hell was going on.

I'd found and mapped Acacia's security system, bypassed the stuff I couldn't avoid, but it was all aimed at what Acacia and Belladonna called *breathers*. There were more heat sensor and motion detection systems. There were pressure-sensitive sensors in most doorways, break-glass detectors, photo-electric sensors in the armored walls of her bedroom-crypt—which was at least a proper safe room. If anybody broke in during the day they'd have a hell of a time getting to her before the paid security arrived.

But it hadn't stopped me at all. It wouldn't have stopped any vampire, so why wasn't she—

I laughed. It was too easy to forget that my opposites didn't always know what I knew. Traditional vamps had the compulsion against uninvited entry; public spaces were fine, but they needed an invitation from a resident of a home. If Acacia or her sire owned the house, and had never invited another vamp onto the premises, then so far as they were concerned the place was vampire-proof.

I smiled ferally; until my nemeses learned about supervamps, I had a secret advantage. They weren't protecting themselves because they thought I couldn't *be* here.

Left free to move on to stage two, I went over the place *again*.

Bright side, if Emerson had surveillance on her it didn't include police bugs. A sweep showed no listening devices for me to work around. On the other hand, the place was beginning to bother me.

The house had been furnished by a professional decorator. Old-style wood and velvet chairs and couches matched the trim and wainscoting on the walls. Chandeliers would light the high-ceilinged parlor, living room, and dining room when company came. The living room itself was large enough to comfortably hold twenty or so guests, and had been arranged to provide different conversation-nooks. The high-quality and overstocked bar showed a history of entertaining.

And there were no "vampire" touches anywhere; even Acacia's "crypt" was just a very fancy bedroom.

I looked in her walk-in closet just to make sure I had the right house. It was hers—they'd killed a lot of cows to fill her wardrobe. But there were also upscale dresses and gowns, Cape Cod casual outfits, stuff *Hope* would be comfortable in but hardly fit Acacia. I was back to *what is going on*?

I put the mystery aside; I could always ask her later.

Her closet made the perfect waiting spot. The walk-in held her vanity mirror, and the door opened away from it; lurking behind the door was a cliché for a reason. The closet ceiling even had a panel giving access to the attic and I unlocked it, opened it a crack to allow me a quick escape if I decided to no-go the snatch at the last second.

Again according to Darren, Acacia haunted the club only three or four nights a week and only until around three in the morning. Then she might wander but was always home a couple hours before dawn. Darren and Leroy had obviously been watching her to see if she led to their V-Juice source—did they and Emerson's boys trip over each other? *This could all get very Keystone Cops real quick.* Smiling at the thought, I went back to the front of the house to watch the street.

She didn't bring meals home with her, but whatever was going on here was interesting to Emerson; after long minutes watching, I spotted his surveillance team. An off-white sedan a little ways down the street on the cemetery side had been there when I drove by earlier. Now it bobbled as whoever was inside shifted. Excellent.

My burner phone buzzed and I read Dupree's text: *They left the club.* They? Well, I probably had hours yet. Finding a luggage set, I packed. Toiletries, underwear, several sets of clothes; if the police searched they would find evidence of a voluntary departure. I slid the suitcases under the bed, leaving one empty, and looked for personal items—pictures, letters, anything she wouldn't want to leave if she wasn't coming back. There weren't any.

I was taking the third turn around the bedroom to make sure I hadn't missed anything when the inside alarm system gave the quiet chime that said it had been turned off. Sooner than I'd expected, but *game on.*

Sliding my kit behind her gowns, I kept only the two

stakes Darren had provided me. I hadn't been lying when I'd told Bobby how unreliable stakes were in a straight-up fight. I wasn't expecting a *fight*, but I'd asked Darren for some serious stakes hoping he wouldn't just send me a sharpened two-by-four or chair leg.

Someone had put a *lot* more thought into these than I had. Made out of African Blackwood, they were so dense they'd sink in water even without the steel cores drilled into them. Each was a foot long, nearly as thin as a chopstick and sharpened to a needle point. Their hilts were wrapped with porous surgical tape to insure a no-slip grip even if my hand got covered in blood. He'd included instructions: the eye-hooks at the base of each stake would let me hide them by tying a heavy thread through the eyes and hanging them down my sleeves—a quick jerk to break the threads and I'd be ready to go.

Voices on the stairs. *Voices.* She wasn't yakking on her cell phone. I could see a good slice of the bedroom from where I stood ready to slide behind the closet door, or behind her coats if I needed time.

A male voice. Darren was wrong; she'd brought dinner home. The knob on the bedroom door turned, and *he* laughed dazedly, enthralled—a laugh I recognized.

Paul.

What the hell?

Chapter Eighteen

"The evil which I would not, that I do. Who shall deliver me from the body of this death?"

Romans 7: 19,24.

I was going to kill him. I was going to kill *Emerson. Off the bloodsucker beat, my cold dead ass.* I would make sure they never found the bodies.

I slid the second stake into my boot, held the first in a backward grip along my arm, and tried to see. The bedroom mirror gave me a safe partial view from the dark closet. Paul was back in his chains and leather, fake ankh tattoo in place. His neck sported a purpling hickey, and her cheeks were flush with too much blood. *Crap.*

They clinched, she popped all his buttons, he peeled her shirt off, they passed beyond the mirror and the bed protested their landing. Had he been pale? How much blood had she taken? She laughed, and he said something.

Slow. Too slow, like he'd had too much to drink. Damn it to hell, he was enthralled, completely vamped. Silence. I risked a look. Paul stared at the ceiling—her face in his neck, feeding *again*.

Couldn't I have *one* night go as planned?

Five ghosting sideways steps, stake swinging up, down. From behind the best shot was under the fifth rib beneath the scapula, her bowed back gave me a perfect frame—and I *missed*. She shrieked and arched, the stake point grinding on a front rib.

I lost my hold, screamed my own frustration and leaped on her as she whirled, fumbled in my boot for the second stake—and hit the wall hard enough to shake my bones, head wrenched half-around by her backhand. Pumped full as she was, she hit like a brick.

Paul saved me, not that he meant to. When she screamed his arms reflexively spasmed tight around her waist—she half-lifted him off the bed, but couldn't go to mist with him attached. I could, and danced in and back out as she tried to track me. Her eyes went wide and then blank as the second stake bit, two ribs below her bra cup and this time I nailed it.

Paul sank back, eyes dilated, shocked into confused immobility by the sudden screaming confusion. Blood poured from Acacia's interrupted bite.

"*Chèr?*"

I threw Acacia aside without a thought, clamped my mouth on his spouting wound and drank. He arched with a rattling sigh as I drew deep, sealed the holes, lay across his bloody chest panting for no reason.

That was... Looking away, I made sure Acacia hadn't moved before giving myself enough room to check Paul.

Blood, his and hers, covered his neck and torso. His pulse beat light but steady, and his idiot-smile made me want to smack him. Repeatedly.

Ask a guy to give you space...

"Jacky?"

Not an observation, just stupid wonder. He might not vamp easy, but he was down deep now and I thought faster than I ever had in my life. Grabbing his face, I locked our eyes. "You two had a great time, Paul, *alone.* She rocked your freaking world, now go to *sleep.*" His eyes slammed shut and he dropped into dreamland so hard he probably bounced.

I sat back, still feeling the need to pant like a winded sprinter, and looked at the mess.

Well, *hell.*

When you're up to your neck in it you move *carefully.*

A radio search showed no transmitters on Idiot Boy. What the hell had he been *doing*? Had Emerson been lying, or was Paul off the reservation? If this was an operation... I was hosed. Emerson would be coming through the door any minute. If this was Paul on his own, trying to *help* me, then maybe The Plan still had a chance. The cops staking out the place might not have even realized she'd brought one of their own home for dinner.

Great. Let's go with that. Okay, time to move.

I retrieved my kit and unrolled the plastic sheets. Duct

tape secured the second stake in its hole, and I pulled and cleaned the first. Blood loss was already returning Acacia to the temperature of death; her consciousness in suspension, she flopped like the fresh corpse she was when I taped her and rolled her up in layers of plastic.

I found the linen closet and pulled fresh sheets, dumped Paul on more plastic, stripped and made the bed. Then I looked at Paul.

Dammit. *When I pictured tonight, I didn't see any bathhouse scenes.*

Cursing some more, I stripped to my underwear. The corset was ruined anyway, sticky with blood, and Acacia could spare something. Stripping Paul down to his boxers, I carried him into the bathroom and propped him under the shower. Washing his hair and scrubbing with a loofa got the blood off his... muscles. Toned country-boy muscles, warm, alive and *stop that.*

Back into the bedroom. Pull back the sheets, bounce around on the bed, twist, generally muss things up. Strip Paul, eyes *up,* drop him on the bed and roll him onto his stomach, pillows on the floor, strategically lay the top sheet while *not* checking his tight butt. I dropped his wet boxers by the shower.

Paul snorted in his sleep, rolled to spread out over the bed. He looked...satisfied. It might work. He might believe the scene I'd set for him, at least long enough for me to get the job done.

And he's never going to forgive me.

Still no Emerson.

Finding Acacia's cellphone, I sent the agreed-on text and got an answer back: *I'm coming.* Raiding her closet should have been fun, but I was in a hurry. A pair of black denim shorts and a stretchy athletic shirt later, I shook out the blonde wig—a little worse for wear from being crunched in my kit—and added some of her favorite lipstick. Blood-red, of course.

The front doorbell rang. The bags! As much as I had to trust Dupree, if he came up here and saw his sister all mummified he might not go through with it. I pulled the packed bags out from their hiding place and down the stairs as the bell rang again.

Let him wait—I *wanted* him seen for this.

Opening the door, I caught Dupree mid-knock. Typical guy; the doorbell works, you *hear* it work, but maybe a knock will work better? Throwing my arms around him, I pulled him inside before he could stiffen.

"What?"

"Your family isn't huggy?" I snarked.

"Oh, yeah. Is she here?"

I handed him the biggest bag. He staggered a bit. "What's this full of? Books?"

"Does she read? Makeup, lots of makeup. And shoes, clothes, underwear... And we're on a schedule, remember? She's running?"

"Right. But she's fine?"

I ground my teeth. "Yes, Dupree, she's fine. Now we need to make sure I have time to make her *better*?"

Maybe he was the kind of guy who was only all together

when it was hitting the fan. I pushed him at the door.

Out on the front porch, I looked around. Really looked, let anyone watching see me look. *C'mon boys, see Jane run.* Dupree had parked his truck just outside the front gate and he tossed his bag in back, helped me do the same before we piled in. He started up, pulled away from the curb, and I watched the mirror.

The sedan followed. *Yes!* I handed him Acacia's cell. "Remember—"

"Keep it on, but don't answer any calls, right."

I nodded. "I'll call *you* when it's time to come back."

"Ma'am?" He looked straight ahead, both hands on the wheel.

"Hmm?" I adjusted his mirror, kept my eyes on our tail. The sedan followed us through two turns as we headed west, then left us as we picked up a second tail, this one a blue compact. They were working it like professionals.

"Why are you really doing this?"

"Because she'll lead me to my target, Dupree, don't get any ideas. I'm not a good Samaritan; whatever mess she's in, she got herself there with her own dumbassedness."

He snuck a look, grunted—whatever that meant—and I'd had enough. I took off the wig, cracked the window.

"Remember—"

"Don't stop, take the fastest road, when I get home pull the truck into the garage and close the door... I've got it all. Anything else?"

A three hour drive, two in sunlight now. He still didn't look happy, and I groaned inside, thought about what Hope would do. *People stuff.*

"Steph will be fine, Robert." I patted him on his solid upper arm. "I promise. One day, two, and you'll be picking her up for real, okay? Get the rest of your posse out of town, fort up. If the headless hoodsmen have an in with the police, they might be coming after you now."

He nodded with another sharp grunt, but smiled a little at the possibility that his part of the plan might have some danger. I managed not to laugh. *Boys.*

"Right," he said. "So get going."

I cracked the window and went to mist. Drifting out into the street and spreading thin, I watched the tailing car pass right through me, waited until both were out of sight, and turned east to retrace our route. Now for the *tricky* part.

Father Graff looked way too calm for someone catching a ride in a car with a body in the back. But then, he *had* served in some interesting places.

"And how are you, *mein kinde?*" Not a trivial question. I ignored it, checking my mirrors again as I turned the corner. Nobody had followed me from Acacia's, and it looked like nobody had followed him.

"Thank you again, Father. This isn't—"

"Saving a soul is always the duty of the Church. Mostly of course, this is done by word, example, and the outstretched hand. But against powers that rob souls of their own sacred volition?" He looked stern. Well, *more* stern.

"Thank you." I left it at that. Turning onto Decatur, I keyed open the garage. Inside, mindful of the stake, I extracted my kit and threw Acacia over my shoulder.

"This is our patient?" was all Father Graff said as I led him through the building to the security room. I rolled my eyes.

"No Father, this is— Whoa!"

Casper had expressed himself. All over the walls.

He'd stuck to his theme; *Get out* had been expressed redundantly in engine oil on every bare surface, carved into the plaster with something handy when the oil ran out. The Ouija board sat in one corner, the slider gone who knows where (probably used to carve the wall). The camera wasn't on its tripod and I wasn't about to take the time to search for the pieces.

"This is not how you left it?"

I shrugged. "Roommate troubles. I may have to do a little cleaning."

"Indeed." He set down his own bag and began rummaging. I pushed the tripod aside and lowered Acacia to the cement floor before checking the security system. No outside alerts, at least, and no record of access; the place was still safe. By some definitions.

Vampire powers make no physical sense, but then neither do our limitations. Why does being physically bound to something too heavy to take with us keep us from going into mist ourselves? Being handcuffed to Emerson's interrogation room table had really meant that only a few square inches of my skin had been in contact with it, so why would it have stopped me? Without the cuffs, I could have lain down on the table and still misted away. Unless I *grabbed* the table—then I wouldn't have gone anywhere. Which made the limitation more metaphysical than physical; contact didn't inhibit us, connection with intent did.

So the first thing was to make sure Acacia had a serious connection with something heavy. Like a motorcycle engine block.

While Father Graff hung crosses, sprinkled the floor and walls, and recited unintelligible Latin, I duct taped and chained Acacia to the abandoned engine block. I used so much tape that the chains were almost redundant, but they made me feel better; she'd fed recently—overfed, from the nearly-pink color of her cheeks—which meant if she got loose she'd outmuscle me.

But we weren't going anywhere.

"I am finished, *mein kinde*," Father Graff reported, closing the book of liturgy and crossing himself.

"The hatch to the sewer?"

"Done also—there will be no escape for her there."

"Thank you, Father." The little wooden crosses made an odd contrast to all the *Get Outs*—most of them now even more drippy, smeared by the liberally sprinkled holy water. I shook my head; Casper would have to wait his turn. I tossed Father Graff the key. "Now I need you to leave. Please bless the door once you've locked it."

He caught the key without thinking, but didn't move.

"Kinde—"

"Please Father, this isn't an exorcism. Helping her isn't in the power of your faith."

"But I may be of help to you." He said evenly. "When a child of light walks in darkness, my duty is clear."

I straightened up. "I will carry you out, Father, and lock the door myself." He looked me in the eyes with no fear of influence, and accepted it with a sigh.

"I will go no further than the door."

"Thank you."

He retrieved his bag and left us, closing the door behind him. I waited until I heard the *clack* of the deadbolt seating itself, and pulled away the plastic covering Acacia's face. Her open eyes stared, sightless.

Shutting them on impulse, I drew a deep, needless breath, and pulled out the stake.

This was going to suck.

Chapter Nineteen

My revenge is just begun! I spread it over centuries, and time is on my side. Your girls that you all love are mine already; and through them you and others shall yet be mine - my creatures, to do my bidding and to be my jackals when I want to feed.

Bram Stoker, *Dracula*.

I knew the moment Acacia went from being an inanimate corpse to an animated one, something with a will inside. Her eyes snapped wide and her entire body jerked uselessly, mummified as she was, and she took a reflexive, hissing breath as the pain of the open wound bit. The hiss became a wail when, twisting her head, she couldn't look anywhere without seeing a cross. She finally scrunched her eyes closed.

"Stephanie?" I said softly. She gasped again and her eyes flew open. I knelt astride her outstretched legs, shoulders and back eclipsing the cross directly behind me.

"Jacky? Why did you—no! I wasn't going to hurt him!"

"Of course not, Stephanie." *Just half-drain him, you greedy witch.* I kept it out of my voice, focused on channeling a stern Grams. "May I call you Steph?"

"No! She's dead!"

"So's Jacky, dead for years. Acacia's fine then. And Paul's fine, so we're fine."

"Then..." Her eyes drifted to the cross-covered walls, snapped back to my face as she shuddered. "We're okay? You can let me go?" She tried to smile.

I shook my head. "Nope. We're both stuck in here together until I get what I want. Then the nice priest who redecorated for me will let us out. Understand?"

"No." Her voice got small, thready, and now I just felt sick. She wasn't a fighter, wasn't *hard*, beyond what her condition made her—just somebody's tool. Taking breath for words, she flinched again. "I'm bleeding."

"I know. It'll pass." I pulled up my borrowed shirt. "I got a matching one." The twisted mark of Dupree's stake was fading fast, but still visible in the bright light of the room's bare bulb. Her eyes widened.

"Your brother did that, after he found you and you didn't recognize him. Thought I'd sired you and staking me would free you. Brotherly love is nice." I pulled the shirt back down. "Of course he missed."

"I never saw Rob! What do you *want*?"

Gotcha. Emerson would have been surprised to hear that, but I had to work to keep the relief out of my voice. "I want to know about your drinking habits—where you got your first drink, to be specific. Who gave it to you, who you fed yourself, who helped you turn." I leaned in, just a little, whispered almost in her ear. "Make me happy, and I'll forget all about what you did to Paul, what your brother did to me. You'll wake up in your own bed, I promise." She jerked her head away.

"I won't!"

I sat back.

"Then we're stuck here together. You know it won't kill us, right? I'm slow but I've been catching up—I know what will happen; we'll get really, really *thirsty*, but you can't get to me and I've got the willpower to keep from draining you. So we'll just dry out, get weak. One night, two, maybe three and then when day comes we'll go to sleep together and won't wake up, not unless someone finds us and *gives* us blood. We could sleep in here forever, or at least until someone looking to buy the property opens the door. When they find us, they'll probably just bury us, so that will be fine."

I kept my tone light, reasonable, like I was discussing how warm the nights were getting, as her eyes darkened with horror and she tried to twist away.

"No! No! *Why*?"

"Because your friends are trying to kill me. Because they tried to kill Grams. Because somebody is ripping people's throats out and that just isn't right. Do you remember your cousin, Richard? He died hard last night, because he was trying to help you. Your friend almost got

Robert. Blood all over the walls... you should have been there—you'd have been drooling."

"He would never—"

"Don't say never, Acacia. He *tried*. We're parasites, we have to be, but once we start *killing*, then they're all just blood-sacks to us."

I stood and stretched, giving her space. "I need his name, *Stephanie*. Who turned you and how? Unless you tell me, your brother is a messy corpse. He won't stop trying to help you, he won't stop coming, and they'll gut him like an animal. But that's okay, right? We'll be asleep by then, anyway."

Despite the tears she didn't break down, but I hadn't expected her to. I hadn't even applied a touch of influence yet; first she had to understand our situation, had to know the way *out*. So I gave her time, checking on the GPS tracker I'd dropped in Dupree's truck.

The epad app showed him well west of town now, and nobody was beating down my door yet. So the cops *thought* they knew where Acacia was. Maybe. And Acacia's master didn't know she was missing yet. Maybe. When he realized she was gone, he might fall for the same play the cops had—and head right for Dupree.

Robert Dupree might have bought himself his own little Killing Night, but he'd known that.

"You're wrong."

I barely heard her. Turning around, I came back to sit by the engine block. She craned her head to look at me. "He wouldn't do that. He couldn't do that."

169

"So tell me who he is. If he didn't, then he's safe."

"I can't. People don't understand him."

Now I locked eyes with her, pushed. "So make me understand."

Without a thought, she hit me with all the influence she had. "He's *good*," she whispered and I loved the guy, whoever he was. "You're all so *beautiful*, so magic, I wanted that, lots of us do. But you wouldn't *let* us, you kept it to yourselves!"

I hunched against the warm waves of adoration coming off her and managed to choke out the question I'd bet everything to ask. "How? How did he help you?"

And her story spilled out. Blood in wineglasses that made them strong and made them sick. Drinking each night, until only the blood made them feel human. Days in a long, dark room barely moving, even to clean themselves. *He* was always there, pouring the blood, comforting, promising, as more and more of them disappeared—"gave up and went back to their dead animal lives," he said.

Only the strong remained to die and be reborn as his children, and how could they not love him? It was *good* and it was *right*, and I wanted to love a man I didn't know and I screamed and scuttled away until my back hit the wall by the door.

Acacia laughed, eyes shining. "See? *See*? He gave us what we needed."

I gagged, tasting blood. Her eyes burned with a pure belief I remembered.

Waking up in illuminating darkness, feeding off the victims he brought me, eager to do anything, be anything he wanted.

There were no words.

She wasn't me, and this wasn't influence-magnified Stockholm Syndrome, an escape from *fear* into mindless love and worship. I'd bitten the inside of my lip in my mad scramble backwards, and now I swallowed repeatedly. Finally able to think again, I looked away, blocking out her sporadic giggles and the sick adoration that beat at me.

And I'd sealed myself in with *that*?

I held onto Dupree's claim of his sister's memory-lapse—which she'd pretty much confirmed from the other direction; she might have been willing, but *He'd* still eaten her completely. She'd been a clueless wannabe, *not* a sociopath, before her sire got ahold of her. I hoped.

Ignoring her, I retrieved my epad, brought up Paul's files—the autopsy pictures of the seven V-Juice overdose victims they'd identified. Five girls, two boys, pale, hollow faces, decently closed eyes. Someone had even straightened their hair to return a little dignity. All the girls were blondes, like Acacia and Belladonna.

"Is Bell one of your sisters?" I asked without thinking, and looked up in time to see her mouth twist with disgust. No, then; He wouldn't let her be jealous of any fellow sisters in his harem. Which didn't mean she wasn't a co-conspirator.

"How many?"

She looked at me blankly, her smothering influence

fading as my question broke her focus.

"What?"

I relaxed, but didn't push back. "How many gave up? How many weren't strong enough for his blood? Do you remember their names?" I forced myself to sit back down beside her, extended the epad so she could see as I flipped through the pictures.

The first drained all the pink from her cheeks, the fourth made her gasp and turn her head away.

"And these are just the ones the police found dumped. There are random ODs, too."

"ODs?"

"Too much of whatever meth-cocktail is in the blood. You think *vampire* blood makes you strong? It's not even ours. What was her name?"

"Vivian. I mean—"

"That's the goth name she used?"

She nodded, eyes tearing. "She didn't— Something must have happened to her after—"

"They were all found stripped and mummified in plastic sheets. Someone kept this batch in an old restaurant freezer—probably didn't want them decomposing one by one before they got rid of them all together. The power company found them, tracing illegal power usage."

"They can't be—"

"The police thought it was just someone covering for a designer-drug gone toxic," I said gently. "Checking their stomach contents turned up the ingested blood. Pig blood.

Your sire *drugged* you, Acacia. A lethal meth-mix that hooks you fast and burns you up. Sooner or later a dose will kill anybody. Or turn the *lucky* ones. How many more are there?"

"Just five—" She caught herself, but I'd been slowly piling on the influence since sitting back down. *These are real, I'm telling the truth, you can believe me.* Really just a projection of my own certainty—she believed that I believed.

"I work with the police, Acacia." *True.* "And I need to find out who poisoned these kids and stuffed them in bags." *True.* "If it's not the man who made you, I need to know who it is." *Absolutely true.*

"*No.* He would *never.*" Absolute certainty so deep it almost drowned me. I hung on.

"Then who?" *Help me.* "Who could get to all of them?" *Help them.* "Why kill them this way and are there others?" *Help them.* "Please tell me something that makes sense!" *Help me save them!*

She started to cry and I made myself sit back, let her mind work on it. "Where was Vivian from?"

"N-New York." She sniffed.

"That's a long way to sleep in a freezer. Friend?"

"Our online fang club. When I told everyone I was coming here she wanted to join me. We shared a room 'til they found us. When she left..."

"Did she tell you she was leaving?"

"No. I woke up one night and they told me she'd changed her mind, gone home..."

"Why do you think they lied?"

"S-something must have happened to her. They didn't want to worry us while we were turning."

"So tell me about her."

She did, while I listened and pushed where I could. And it wasn't *working*. Her eyes swam as she talked about Vivian. Dammit, stripped of the pose and attitude, Acacia was *nice*. Clueless but nice, and her niceness was a shield. She was like Hope but without the backbone or intelligence—she couldn't imagine evil in anyone she loved and her enthrallment reinforced that. Her mind danced around it, invented excuses, reasons somebody else must have done those awful things.

And I couldn't push her past that—she could feel and resist that kind of attack just like I had. I'd never overcome her enthrallment before Emerson realized I'd suckered him and broke down the door. Or her sire got to Grams or Dupree. I could see it coming, certain as sunrise.

If she wasn't a vamp I could just make *her* forget all this like I did for Marco—

Wait. Forget. I clutched my head.

"Acacia," I interrupted her. "Don't you want to find out who's responsible for all this?"

"Yes! I want it to all go away!"

She wanted *me* to go away, to stop threatening her world. But I could work with that. I leaned in, kept my voice low, urgent. "You said you don't remember your brother running into you at Angels." *Why?* "So somebody's memory has been messed with—yours or his. He wouldn't lie." *He loves you.* "Maybe somebody played with his mind and sent him after me." *He's a victim.* "Or maybe he told you something important and the vamps trying to kill him don't want you to remember." *Help him!*

She nodded spastically, my influence reinforcing every sisterly instinct. "So what can I do?"

"If he talked to you then you need to remember. I can help you, if you trust me."

My plan rested on her sire being as psychotic as Tommy had been, but between his poisoning kids in job lots to make a few devoted vamps, and his escalating to ripping people's throats out, it looked like a safe bet.

So now I just had to find the nerve to do something I'd sworn I'd never do. This was *really* going to suck.

Chapter Twenty

Only beware of this, that thou eat not the blood, for the blood is the soul.

Deuteronomy 12:23.

A hundred magic traditions and every old religion recognized the significance of blood. I tried to ignore all that ritual crap, but even for me, to bring all my influence to bear on a subject I needed a blood connection. And like I'd told Emerson, between vampires the willing *donor*, not the donee was dominant. I was pretty sure there was some sexual allegory there that I really didn't want to look at.

Damn nineteenth-century romantic writers.

Acacia's eyes widened when I unsheathed my Arkansas toothpick, got even wider when I laid it against my left wrist and sliced. I raised my arm before I could lose my resolve and she lunged forward against her chains, mouth wide to catch the red that bloomed against my pale skin. Her lips suctioned to my wrist and she bit.

Oh. My. God. I laughed as burning frost danced through my veins, slow, languorous, creeping up my arm to spread until I could feel the direct connection between her mouth and my unbeating heart.

Now I understood, and I gave Paul, and Hope, and every other voluntary donor I'd ever had a silent apology as I counted. Forcing myself to break the connection, I ignored her hungry gasp. Blood ran down her chin and my wrist until I sealed the wound with my own lips.

That was... Later. I'd think about it later. Now I steadied myself and took hold of Acacia's face, looked into her wide, dilated eyes. "Are you ready?"

She managed to nod and that was all I needed. "Then remember. Remember *everything.*"

She screamed and twisted away, head hitting the engine block behind her with a sickening thud. She vomited up the blood she'd just had from me as I scrambled to unchain her. She kept screaming as I sawed at her plastic and duct tape shroud; cut free, she wrapped her arms around her head, curling up as I desperately worked to free her legs.

Pulling her feet free, I threw the knife aside.

"Acacia! Acacia! Dammit *Stephanie!*" The screams turned to siren wails—broken only for air and way beyond what anyone living could project without coughing up their vocal cords in bloody chunks. I grabbed her arms. "Steph, stop!" The wailing cut off like all the air had left her lungs, but her eyes and silent mouth screamed.

I'd never been a touchy-feely person, even *before*, but I pulled her in and wrapped her cold body in my cold arms. How could I possibly have forgotten this part?

"I know, Steph," I whispered into her knotted hair. "You want to die, right *now*. If you're dead you can stop *seeing* it, you can stop knowing what you are."

"Kill me." She choked, tried again. "Please." Her nails dug divots into my back.

I pulled away so she could see my face. "I'll kill him instead. Promise."

It was the easiest promise I'd ever made.

Watching a priest try to minister to a grief and guilt-stricken vampire should have been funnier. I busied myself taking the little wooden crosses off the walls, then left Father Graff with Acacia and wandered upstairs. We'd passed into day sometime during the drama, and dust motes danced in sunbeams muscling their way through the old shutters. I sat down to watch them, back to the wall. They made pretty death rays, and I hypnotized myself with golden sparks of dust until my burner phone buzzed, summoning me back downstairs.

The scene had barely changed; Father Graff gripped Acacia's folded hands as she prayed almost silently, moving her lips and twitching over words that obviously *hurt*. He held a rosary and she kept her eyes fixed on the cross she carefully didn't touch. I should have realized she was Catholic; most Cajun were, being originally French Canadians.

"Jacqueline," he said. "Stephanie has made a full

confession, and now there are some things she needs to tell you. What was done to her."

It was so much worse than I'd imagined.

She told her story with a flat, dead voice, a wrenching whisper as my epad recorded in dictation mode. The one thing she couldn't tell me was who *He* was; he'd always worn the Mardi Gras mask and hood that seemed to be his little group's trademark. But I'd been wrong; Acacia hadn't been his enthralled follower—she'd been his *toy*.

I forced myself to ask clarifying questions, get numbers and dates, recorded everything while trying to keep the screaming inside my head. Finished, she sagged bonelessly into the sleep of the dead. I could feel the heaviness of the sun myself—probably the only thing keeping me from committing some serious property damage. That, and knowing she'd given me enough information to find the monster.

With a final prayer, Father Graff put away his rosary.

"Will she rest?"

I sighed. "Dreams are for the living, Father. She'll be okay 'til dusk. She *really* needs her family, but her brother is buying us time as a decoy. And if *He* gets his hands on her again—"

My cell phone rang, Paul's number blinking on the screen.

"Are you going to answer?" Father Graff asked as I stared at the number.

"I—excuse me, Father." I stepped away and gingerly held the phone to my ear, feeling ridiculous. "Paul?"

"What the *hell* is going on?"

I managed to get Acacia cleaned and re-dressed before Paul arrived; Father Graff stepped out to give us privacy and meet Paul when he came in through the garage. It helped that she looked like an anemic narcoleptic instead of a murder victim, but not much.

"What the hell are you doing?" were the first words out of his mouth.

Okay, she looked like a fresh and well-dressed corpse. Her blonde locks were a rat's nest, and plastic sheets on a concrete floor didn't make a convincing bed.

"*She's* sleeping. I wish I was. How did you know?"

His eyes burned and his fists visibly twitched. He looked mad enough to forget his upbringing and take a swing at me. I wanted him to; after this morning, a fight would be fun.

My provoking smile didn't help; he almost *growled*. "When Emerson wakes me up and asks where the girl *they* were watching and *I* went home with is, I know where to look."

"Woke you up?"

"In my skin in Acacia's *bed*. Personally."

I let my smile widen. "You woke up with Emerson in Acacia's bed?"

"Don't—" He clawed his hair, visibly took hold of his temper.

"Surveillance saw me go home with Acacia. Then they saw Acacia leave with her brother. Since he and his cousins are out on bail, they had to get permission to go back to

Marksville until the trial if there ever is one. Emerson had the state police out there verify Dupree's arrival, but he couldn't produce Acacia and a traffic camera near city limits showed he left town without a passenger."

I had to ask. "Did you go home with Acacia—you know—voluntarily?"

"*No.*" He was almost growling again. "Didn't think she could vamp me, bought her a drink, was telling how you and I weren't together anymore. Covering for you. Then I woke up. Naked. With my *boss* poking me."

"Really? I didn't think he swung that way."

"Dammit Jacky!"

"What did you tell Emerson?"

"What I knew, which was jack crap."

"Then how did you—oh. You *changed*, didn't you?" I mimed claws. All that trouble to dress the scene...

"In the bathroom. Your smell was all over my *boxers*, Jacky! And the towels. And on *me*. What the hell?"

"And you didn't—"

"Emerson thinks Acacia's on the run, but he's not stupid. He hasn't forgotten about the hotel, and he's coming to check the safe house *he* approved—doesn't even need a warrant."

Oh shit. I froze.

At least I'd had the sense to take the blood soaked sheets with me... Which Emerson would find if he searched the Cadi. *Dammit.* The fun of a pissed-off Paul was gone, and rising panic burned around the edges of my creeping daylight lethargy. Emerson could be here any minute and if I was still awake I would find out how truly pissed off he could get. With bloody sheets and plastic, stakes that would shine bright blue in the forensics lab (you *can't* get all blood-trace out of wood)...

And yet here was Paul, one step ahead of his own team. Why? *Think about that later, girl.*

I looked down at Acacia, laid out like Sleeping Beauty where anyone could do *anything.* No way Emerson was finding me like that. *Okay. Okay. Be elsewhere.* But where was safe? When in doubt, simplify the situation.

"Father?" I called. Father Graff had hung back by the door, wisely not wanting to get in the way if shots were fired. "Would you accept a request for sanctuary?" I turned to Paul. "Acacia hasn't been charged with anything. Right?" He shook his head.

"She hasn't done anything wrong that we know of *yet.* Not like *interfering in a police investigation.*"

"If the Church can keep her safe for now, Father, I can take care of myself."

He nodded understanding. "It would be our duty, given what she has been through." He smiled grimly. "A duty we can fulfill easily. Her needs—"

I kept my eyes on Paul. "I can send you someone who can see her needs looked after."

He nodded again. "Then we should go."

"Jacky. *Chèr* ..."

I looked away. "I'll explain later, Paul. *Please.* I'm not sleeping here, and right now there's nobody else I trust to take us through sunlight."

Chapter Twenty One

Blood strengthens vampires, and with enough blood in them they can easily stay awake past dawn. But a vampire's sleep is the sleep of the dead; until they wake at or close to sundown, they are as unresponsive as a corpse—and as helpless. This is why most vampires prefer that their resting places be either secret or very secure, and prefer to sleep alone.

Dr. Mendel, *The Psychology of Supernaturals.*

I left most of my gear, everything except the forensic evidence and of course my guns and pointy things, since I didn't want to give Emerson the idea that *I* was running, too. Looking at the walls, I decided Casper's smeared graffiti would give the detective enough to think about. Wrestling with my growing panic at Emerson's expected arrival, I took a moment to find the smashed camera and pull its memory chip. If Casper had "said" anything before throwing his tantrum, the boys in the University of New

Orleans' supernatural studies department might be able to learn more about him. *I* didn't have time for it.

Paul and I rolled Acacia up in more plastic and stowed her in the Cadi's trunk. I wrapped myself in the emergency blanket before climbing in and spooning up behind her.

Unlike the last daytime drive, now I had to fight to stay awake; I couldn't sleep 'til I was *safe*. Finally I felt us bump up onto the driveway back to the Archives Building. Paul called "Cover!" before opening the trunk to heft Acacia out and shut it again. A couple of minutes later we were back on the street. I tried to count the stops and corners, but lost track and his quick park surprised me out of my half-daze.

I pulled the blanket's edges in around me, heard Paul's knock before the trunk opened and jerked reflexively as he felt around my feet and up my legs, tucking everything tighter.

"Are you ready, *chèr*?"

I nodded inside my cover, cleared my throat. "If you drop me I'll kill you."

"You're welcome. One. Two. Three." He lifted me out, the front gate clanked as he pushed it out of the way, up the steps, thumping on the wood porch, then the door closed behind us. I panicked for no reason at all when he lowered me, got hold of myself when I felt the overstuffed cushions of Grams' couch. I pulled the blanket back before he could, and found myself looking up at a frowning Grams.

"You have been a great deal of trouble, Jacqueline."

Grams had set out the *good* china, with tea for her but with a full pot of coffee brewed from my stash. The heavenly smell competed with the essence of candles and oils and herbs imprinted on the room by her years of client sessions. Grams poured while I got out of the blanket, got my hair out of my face, got my face straight so I could accept a cup with a smile. Sitting on the loveseat by the sofa, Paul accepted his own cup. Pouring a cup of English tea for herself, she sat back in the matching chair and looked at us.

"Are you finished running around?"

Paul looked at me, but I wasn't any help—the taste of roasted Ethiopian shade bean had me blinking desperately, close to tears. It was the coffee, not the cinnamon-lacquered and brocade covered old furniture, or the faded Wedgewood patterned wallpaper, or the mantle full of pictures, or the sight of Grams. Really.

"Jacqueline?"

I swallowed. "Yes, Grams."

"Good. And Detective Negri, you can prevent a repeat of the other day's unpleasantness?" Paul nodded.

"Excellent. I have made up the old servants' quarters behind the kitchen. You can remain and supervise the... protection detail? you have inflicted on my house. With Wesley's blessing, I am sure."

Now Paul blinked. "Wesley?"

"Lieutenant Emerson, young man. I have had quite enough of all this unnecessary perambulation. "

I choked into my cup. *Wesley?* Paul was turning red.

"If the boy wishes to speak to Jacqueline, he may come by after sunset," Grams instructed, then turned to me. "You will be here?"

"I—I will have to go out," I said weakly. "But I can call a cab and be back quickly enough." My tired mind raced. Wesley? The *boy*? There was a story here; too bad I was about to face-plant into Grams' serving set.

She gave me a sharp look and took my cup away.

"Then you had best get to bed."

"Yes Grams," I said meekly. *Bed*, the most beautiful word in the world; just thinking about it half-hypnotized me. Leaving Paul to his fate, I climbed the stairs to my room.

But I didn't crawl into my coffin; instead I fired up my laptop and went through the tedious password process, then transferred the sound file of Acacia's story and my questions. Painfully slow thought added a sketchy assessment with a search and background-check request, and a note to call Father Graff and assist if needed. I clicked the "send" button feeling like I'd lit a fuse. From my desk to my coffin took less than thirty seconds, most of that to lock up my crypt and turn on its alarms. Closing and latching the lid, I exhaled and was gone.

Normally I rose with the sun still on the horizon, on the edge of twilight, but this time Beethoven's ode to night's silver orb serenely marked the sunset as I opened my eyes. One night remained until the dark moon and the Midnight Ball.

So why did I feel so good?

I was home.

Dammit. When did that happen? Less than two months living in an uneasy truce with a prickly Grams as surprised to meet me as I'd been to meet her, and suddenly it was *home.* I groaned, covering my eyes. *There's no place like home. Great.* New Orleans was supposed to be a side trip—a few months paying my debt to the DSA, firmly establishing my new identity, and getting to know family I hadn't known I'd had.

I opened the coffin lid and sat up, ran my fingers through my hair. I was even getting used to the damned box. Sure, the fact that it was basically a custom-made safe covered in wood paneling had something to do with it, but *still.* Once upon a time I'd slept in a bed.

And when did I start calling a cab to order takeout?

I called anyway, then showered and changed like I was late for school, motivated by a text-message left on my phone; Gray wanted to meet me at our usual spot. Feeling like a delinquent teen, I left a text and slipped out through my bedroom window to avoid seeing Grams or Paul. Checker Cabs answered fast and got me to Napoleon House. Ang, my Tibetan driver, was courteous and filling— and my moral slide continued. I doubled the fare.

Gray wore a clean shirt, but there was no other evidence he'd moved between my visits. He looked at me over his paper when I pushed through the crowd and sat down. "Kimie left her boyfriend and moved back to Houston," he said. "Apparently your exit the other night was inspiring."

"Glad I could help." The new waitress avoided us just as carefully, so I assumed Gray had propositioned her at least once and checked his sandwich. He made a show of leaning in and stroking my reluctant hand, passing off a flash drive under cover of creepy-older-man lechery.

"We've removed Stephanie Dupree and the vampire in Lieutenant Emerson's custody," he said caressingly. "Good work."

"*What?*" I jerked my hand back, nearly knocked over my drink. "Ac—Stephanie's a *victim.* How could you—" Gray glanced a warning toward the bar, but I couldn't believe what I'd heard. "She was under the protection of the *Church*!"

He shrugged it off, leaned back. "She'll be a guest at Camp Necessity until we're confident that the trauma she experienced hasn't made her unsafe. And I'm sure our government and the Vatican are even now exchanging very secret recriminations. The other one—well, we need practice deprogramming vampire victims anyway. The DSA is taking over the V-Juice investigation."

I clamped down hard on a scream. Emerson might not blame me. I was just the DSA asset loaned to his department—*yeah, like he's going to believe that*—but I couldn't imagine what Father Graff must be thinking. Or Dupree, who I'd *promised*— Gray had just casually blown up my reason for being here and my fragile network and he sat there smiling and I could *tell* he knew I was imagining kneecapping him with my Desert Eagle. *Just one knee, dammit—he'll heal eventually!*

"*Why?*" was all I managed. It was almost a hiss.

"You're kidding, right?"

"Do I *look* like I'm kidding?"

He leaned close.

"You report a vampire who's just been forced to remember being serially tortured, raped, and killed, and all you ask is that we help *feed* her?" For once his mask slipped and he looked something other than slyly depraved. Then he winked for our audience, leaned in again. "Do you think your priest and his friends could handle her without killing her if she, oh I don't know, went bat shit raving crazy on them?"

I didn't! I survived! I wanted to scream that in his smug, smarmy face. But as horrifying as the admission was, there was no comparison between what my sire had done to me and hers had done to her. In his own sick way, he'd loved me until I killed him. "So you'll lock her up until the shrinks tell you she's *safe*? I've never met one who didn't think we were all just one bad day from a killing spree—at *best*!"

He shrugged that away too. "It's better than a killer vamp on the loose."

"We've *got* a killer vamp on the loose! Did you find what I said to look for?"

"No, and yes. The FBI has two open cases, probably not all of them. One in Detroit, one in Boston. Young blondes, spiked to walls, tortured, raped, exsanguinated. First one nearly a year ago, the second five months ago. Like I said, they probably haven't found all of them—the two they know about were meant to be hid. Nothing after that."

"Sure, because he'd turned *Acacia* then—she's been his victim *three times*. He makes her forget and she's all better in a couple of days! He *recycles*! But he doesn't have her anymore so he'll be looking for a new toy soon!"

"And we'll find him. Not you—you're to back off. We've got someone breeding vamps through better chemistry, and that's a whole level above serial killer. So you're done. Get out of town. When this is over you can go back to trapping kiddy-fang."

You're right; we're done.

I threw my drink at his head and spit in his face, considered lighting the bar on fire on the way out, but as much as he liked the dramatic exit that would be a bit over the top. I made it out of Napoleon's without any vandalism, but fell against the rough and flaking wall, eyes tight shut. Taking deep and useless breaths to keep from screaming, I tried to push away the images Acacia's broken story played inside my head.

"Miss, are you alright?"

I turned away from the wall and the owner of the concerned voice took two steps back and nearly tripped off the low curb.

"*No. Go away.*" It came out a ragged whisper, but I pushed with all the influence I had. The tour bus just missed my Good Samaritan, and I didn't stay to see if he stopped running.

Chapter Twenty Two

How blessed are some people, whose lives have no fears, no dreads, to whom sleep is a blessing that comes nightly, and brings nothing but sweet dreams.

Bram Stoker, *Dracula*.
So your life sucks. Boo hoo.

Jacky Bouchard, *The Artemis Files*.

Paul looked better than someone who had no regular sleep cycle and was too many ounces low had a right to. I hadn't had time to think about his own "special" condition, but now I wondered if it gave him the kind of recuperative powers regular werewolves had. Grams had joined us in the kitchen, listening without comment as I caught him up. It being after her consultation hours, her hair was pulled back in a steel grey bun, her face devoid of its usual arch makeup.

"So that's it?" Paul said finally. "The DSA has dropped you? And taken away our investigation?"

"More like they've cut me loose for now." I kept my eyes on my coffee. The cup steamed fragrantly, but didn't warm my cold hands. "I'm a civilian asset, not an agent, and with my background they don't consider me that reliable." I shook my head when he started to protest. "Not—they know I'd never jam them up. I'm just not... not one of theirs."

The flash drive had included account numbers, plane ticket purchases, and instructions to go back to Chicago. *At least they realize I'm still a target.* More than before, if Emerson's department was as leaky as I thought it was. Acacia's sire had to know that Emerson believed I'd helped her disappear, and with no leads left to follow I was more dangerous to my friends than my enemies now. Dangerous to Grams.

"But they still haven't found him?" Paul couldn't let it go. I'd given him and Grams a sketchy description of Acacia's story. It had been light on the gut-churning details, but still enough to shut down all expression on his expressive face.

"No." I shook my head. "They found the room Acacia—Stephanie—told me about, the place where she and the others were turned. Dead end." Gray had had the decency to include the investigation file with my walking papers, for what good it did. He knew how to do his job; he'd used Acacia's description to define a search, narrowed it down to three locations, and had teams in the doors before lunchtime. They'd found the old lab and the "crypt," but either *He* was done building his vamp army or he'd moved his operation.

It checked with my phone conversation with Leroy (*that* had been as fun as always); the couple of V-Juice dealers he'd been able to "talk to" hadn't just been dead ends—they'd been cut off, selling the last of their inventory.

Leroy. As much as I wanted Acacia's twisted sire dead and ashes, I wanted Leroy's sire nearly as much—and Gray had taken away my bargaining chip with MC...

"When do you leave, child?" Grams lowered her teacup with a gentle clink, bringing me back to the conversation.

"The ticket's for tomorrow night."

"And you'll use it?"

Bouchards run, Grams. Mom did. "I'm at Sable's tonight—I'll let him know he's not escorting me to the Midnight Ball tomorrow. He can't insist if I'm not in town." I looked at Paul, shrugged apologetically. "Don't—"

"Don't tell Emerson 'til you're gone."

"But you'll return?" She might as well have been politely asking when she'd need to change the sheets, but I realized I'd made that decision already.

"When they get him, Grams. Promise."

Her mouth tightened, but she accepted it gracefully with only a nod. I repeated the promise to myself. Maybe I'd be able to keep this one.

To my relief (I *really* didn't want to tell him I knew

about his ass-dimples), Paul seemed to have decided to drop his questions about what happened at Acacia's. He'd stood watch while I slept, for which I was even more grateful; it didn't matter that the contracted professional who'd bled out all over her carpet had managed to slip by Oz and Steve outside, Grams still refused to let strangers invade her home.

Paul drove me to Sable's like it was a normal night, which meant that I left him a block away and arrived out of mist on Sable's doorstep. Henry, Sable's hulking doorman, didn't blink when I changed to flesh right behind a pair of fang fans. I was back in my high waisted and buttoned down skirt outfit that bordered on Gothic Lolita and there was no way I could carry the Desert Eagle, but my poofed skirts hid the Kel-Tec in its thigh holster quite nicely, an advantage I hadn't appreciated before. With the stakes in my boots, I felt confident I could handle anyone jumping me here—not that it was likely.

Anyone could attend Sable's "salons" by RSVP'ing, and he always had at least one or two other vamps in attendance. I had to stay no less than one hour and take at least one "supplicant" before I left—that was our deal. Sable didn't choose for himself until late in the night, when his current Lucy would inform his choices of their good fortune and his small party would retire to his rooms, ending the evening's *festivities*.

Half his choices would be his favorites, but half were always new blood.

Working my way inside, I found the place as stuffy and

crowded as ever. There had to be close to thirty wannabes and fang fans in the parlor, more in the hall. They pressed even tighter tonight; Sable had decided to have his portrait done, so he lounged in his gold leafed chair while the portrait artist worked on his profile. The space blocked off for the artist and his easel, guarded by a velvet rope nobody dared touch, left less room for the rest of us.

Evangeline stood on Sable's right so he'd have someone to talk to, and he held a crystal goblet filled with red wine in his left hand, white flounced sleeves with bloodstone cufflinks and crimson cravat adding color to his black regency outfit. His blond curls were almost as styled as Evangeline's, who looked a little pale under her makeup.

Even my influence couldn't buy me much space, but when I squeezed my way to the front Sable smiled to see me—and frowned minutely when I failed to curtsy, never part of our deal. He put down his glass, kissed Evangeline's hand, and rose to "make a leg" in a showy bow of his own.

"Jacqueline, how good of you to come." The sly bastard hid a smirk as his play forced a half-hearted curtsy out of me. His extended hand forced me to take it, and he planted a lingering kiss on my wrist. A raised eyebrow was his only observation on the nearly invisible line that showed under the edge of my glove, the fast fading reminder of my donation to Acacia.

Behind him Evangeline smile vacuously, the very picture of an empty-headed Lucy.

He released my hand, straightening. "A pleasure, as

always," he whispered. "Will you join our intimate party tonight, my dear?" He added another smile and a touch of influence to the request. Did he think he was being playful?

I lowered my voice. "Would that I could." *Hell no.* "Perhaps another night." *After the sun dies of natural causes.* "Sadly, tomorrow night I must take my leave of New Orleans. I will greatly miss the opportunity to attend the Midnight Ball in your delightful company." Seriously, I'd practiced for Sable's by forcing myself to read regency romance bodice-rippers.

The frown came back. "Trouble? May I be of assistance?"

"Family. Responsibilities. I am sure you understand." I channeled Evangeline and batted my eyes, playing to the audience. If I *ever* told Hope about this, she'd die laughing. Sable accepted it, if only because grilling me on the spot would break our little pantomime, and released my hand with expressions of tragic regret. A regal wave indicated that I was free to snack on his court. *Partake* was the word he used, like a fancy word changed anything.

The menu was broad as always, from barely legal to mid-thirties, anorexic to abundant, in many shades of goth (mostly Regency to Victorian, but no punk). The low light and the room's overuse of red made them look washed out, phantoms enlivened by sparks of color off of theater jewelry. Positioning myself behind the portrait artist let me put my back to the room without being obvious. He really was quite good.

At Angels I would have instantly formed a court, but here most everyone knew that I would only pick one of them while Sable might choose five or six later (I assumed he sipped lightly and paced himself). So they hung close, but the room's center of gravity and the nexus of the crowd's Brownian motion remained the throne. I had fun bouncing them off of me, like an electron-repelling molecule; they would greet me with Regency Speak and bad accents, and I would compliment their costumes and remark on how beautiful the night was while using influence to give them the unconscious willies.

Eventually I acquired a bubble of space, par for the course at Sable's, and could relax a bit. Except I didn't; the entire time I was getting more and more edgy without knowing why. *Finally*, enough time passed that I could eat and run, and I nearly grabbed the girl standing closest to me—an alternately excited and nervous rockabilly goth with Betty Page hair and clunky shoes who showed more imagination than the rest of them despite her nerves. Taking her hand, I pulled us out of the parlor and down the hall in a rush that left a wake of startled babble behind us.

"I—I'm not sure I want to do this," were her first words as I closed the study door.

"That's a shock." I turned and leaned against it, smiling with fang. "I can *make* you want to." I'd been planning on quick, but now I realized I'd picked her for a reason. Her pale skin tone was makeup—she wasn't a serious light-adverse goth—but in the dim light of the table lamp she got paler.

I pushed away from the door and stalked towards her, eyes on her neck. She backed up until the old roll-top desk stopped her short.

"Have you heard of *implied consent*?" I asked conversationally, ignoring her rising panic. "With vampires, implied consent means that if someone like you knowingly goes to a gathering where bloodsuckers like me will be picking up donors, they cannot later claim that they were forced unless there are witnesses to their attempted rejection. The place for that was outside this *private* room." I ended the lecture inches from her neck. Using my arms to frame her, I trapped her against the edge of the desk. Under the perspiration she smelled like lilies, but I ignored my sudden thirst.

"You can't—"

"I just finished telling you I *can*. What do you do when the sun is up?"

"I—I'm a waitress."

"Read a lot?"

"Yes." It was practically a squeak. Looking close, I saw the Betty Page hair was a wig. Raising a hand, I twisted a red lock into view. Betty flinched away.

"I can guess what you read. So tonight is your grand adventure? I hope you're having a good time, because now your only choice is whether you will amusingly resist or relax and... *enjoy it*."

I pushed with the last words, and her eyes widened as her cheeks flushed. She stopped leaning away, and I waited till there was no light between us before dropping the influence. She gave a strangled gasp and shrank away again, starting to cry.

"But I lie," I said softly. "You have one more choice. You can choose to *remember* my kiss, and believe me, there's nothing else like it. It's *very* addictive—you may spend the rest of your life depending on the kindness of strangers like me for a high you won't get anywhere else... Or I can make you forget. You'll feel pretty damn good afterwards—like an endorphin high—without knowing why."

"Please," she said. "Please, I want to go." A hopeless declaration more than a plea. I kissed her on the cheek and stepped back.

"Wonderful. Did you drive or take a taxi? Or did you come with friends?"

It turned out she'd changed and walked from the café where she waitressed, so I called Paul and got us out the side door. Paul picked us up and got directions, without commentary on my companion's tear streaked makeup. I gave a gradually recovering Jenny—she hadn't chosen a goth name—a list of suggestions as he drove. Dancing. Hang gliding. Extreme sports. Anything that meant reading less vamp-lit and getting out more. When we dropped her off outside her apartment she went quietly.

"Rescuing them physically, now?" Paul asked once she'd disappeared inside.

I sighed. "Practicing catch-and-release." I wasn't ready to tell him what I'd decided. No more fang fans, no more courts, just old fashioned felony assault. Paul might have seriously mixed feelings on the issue, but my meals weren't going to come back for seconds anymore. "I'm pretty sure I just burned my bridges with Sable, anyway."

I had no idea how right I was.

Chapter Twenty Three

"All was dark and silent, the black shadows thrown by the moonlight seeming full of a silent mystery of their own. Not a thing seemed to be stirring, but all to be grim and fixed as death or fate, so that a thin streak of white mist, that crept with almost imperceptible slowness across the grass towards the house, seemed to have a sentience and a vitality of its own."

Bram Stoker, *Dracula*.

"Okay, that may have been me."

Jacky Bouchard, *The Artemis Files*.

Once you're thirsty you're thirsty. Paul let me off on Chartres and I found a lonely drug dealer who tasted like he sampled his product. I justified it on the grounds that tomorrow night I'd be on an airplane and I wouldn't want to hunt my first night back in Chicago. Checking the guy's wallet, I stole his fitness club card and made a mental note to let Emerson pass his name to vice.

The small hours of the night were my favorite time, when even the most determined partiers and human predators had mostly gone to bed. The sliver of moon rode low in the sky as I walked the quarter, and I could smell the Mississippi in the wind.

It didn't smell like Lake Michigan.

Really, I walked to prove I could. No other vamps rode the wind, no tails skulked after me. Whatever nastiness Acacia's sire had planned, it wasn't happening tonight and now that the DSA was on the job he couldn't have that many nights left. I hoped. If I was Catholic like Hope, I'd light a thousand candles and pray that the monster wouldn't let them take him "alive". Saints probably didn't answer prayers like that. Or listen to vampires.

I walked up Esplanade as the predawn light washed out the stars. Letting myself in, I passed Legba (Grams let him out to wander the house at night, putting him away when he came back to his room for breakfast). He flicked his tongue at me before gliding away. Grams wouldn't be up until later; working the "night shift" like she did, she'd open her eyes around noon and be ready to see me off when I rose tonight.

In my room I changed into my black nightgown and tied up my hair, debated calling Hope to let her know I was coming, and decided against it. Opening the wall to my crypt, I engaged its security and climbed into my coffin, sealing out the world for another day.

The ear-stabbing wail of the security alarm from hell shattered my breathless sleep, and I smashed my head and knees convulsively trying to sit up. Then my world tipped as somebody pushed my coffin off its stand. *What?* Thoughts slow, I tried to wake up under the weight of the sun, to untangle my dead arms. My coffin rang like a gong, *bounced.* I laughed, snarled. Someone had tried to blow it open.

Which meant they'd penetrated my safe room crypt. Which meant they'd gotten past Paul's security and *Grams.*

I finally found the nightlight, switched it on and realized the side of my coffin had become the floor. I ran my fingers along the edge of the lid. The seal was good, the bank safe quality armor held. A second explosion, distant this time. The coffin tipped again, flipping me on top of the closed lid and raining bits of pressed dirt down on me, then slid to stop hard—against a wall?

My phone had slid somewhere unfindable, I didn't know what was going on, and I realized the weakness of my coffin's design: no vents. It was airtight and I was trapped, even assuming my crypt wasn't open to sunlight now—which might have been the second explosion.

Then my feet started to warm and I realized vents might not be a problem. They were *burning their way in.*

At my *feet?* Why? I ground my teeth, trying to think around the sick screaming rage that filled my head. Grams could be *dead.* If they cut a hole for me I'd take a chance on the sunlight—I could at least pull somebody's spine out while I lit up like a tiki torch.

My phone rang by my head and I scrambled for it, pulled it free of the matting it had snagged in.

"*Jacky?*" Paul's voice, high, intense.

"Yes!"

"*Are you safe?*"

"They're burning through my coffin! What is *wrong* with you?"

"*We're coming! Don't come out!*" He disconnected and I screamed at the air. With a skittering pop and a splatter of burning steel, they breached. I dropped the phone and flailed my bare feet, hissing as spatter burned into my flesh.

I'd rip their arms off, let them see the error of their ways while they bled out. I'd never considered it before, but get a grip and brace a foot against someone's rib cage... A metal pipe poked in by my feet and icy water roared in under high pressure. Water? Were they trying to *drown* me?

I kicked at the pipe out of reflex, but it had a hooked cap that kept me from pushing it out and high-pressure water sprayed over my nightgown-tangled legs. *Water?* I started laughing hysterically. The nightlight shorted out, and when the flow cut off I lay in the dark in maybe three inches of water, screaming and swearing and giggling.

It was easy to lose track of time when I didn't even have a heartbeat to count, but it couldn't have been more than a few minutes before someone flipped my coffin back over, starting me swearing again. I was *so* kicking somebody's ass.

The same someone whacked the lid with what sounded like a crowbar, rhythmically and repeatedly. Paul? He certainly couldn't call—the phone was underwater. If it wasn't Paul I'd get to kill somebody, so, win-win: I threw the bolts, pushed, squinted at the light. *Not* direct sunlight. Paul reached down and grabbed my hand.

"So this is what you look like in the morning?"

Grams wrapped my feet, which was totally unnecessary; the deep pits from the spattered steel were already closing and I certainly didn't feel them. I think it made her feel better.

The hunters had attacked after Grams had gone out with Legba to do a ritual cleansing for a client, and they'd taken down Oz and Steve, non-lethally but with all the silent efficiency of an elite paramilitary team. Killing a vampire was one thing—even in the Big Easy a lot of people thought the only good vamp was a dead one—but killing two *cops*, even off-duty cops, would have brought hell down on them.

Paul had been out meeting Dupree. He'd called him last night without my knowing and Dupree had come back to town, so they'd been just a few blocks away when the security firm monitoring my crypt alarms reported the breach.

Paul acted casual about it, but to me it looked like the two of them had gone crazy trying to reach me. They'd tried to shoot their way in but had been kept away from the crypt until the masked hunters blew a hole in the outside wall to let in the sun. *Then* they'd broken into the house next door—nobody home, *Thank you, God*—and laid fire into the crypt from the second story windows. At that point the hunters had probably thought I was dead (I wasn't *sure* a holy water bath would kill a normal vamp, but it had obviously been their backup plan when they couldn't crack my coffin). They'd bailed out the back and escaped—leaving my heroes to pull me out of my banged-up box, madder than hell, burned, soaked, and covered in garden dirt.

"I don't understand," Dupree said again, watching Grams work. Oz and Steve had been replaced by a new security team, for all the good they were doing, and the rest of us sat in the kitchen. A fire truck and two police cars were parked outside, but no fires had spread and Paul had control of the "crime scene" for now.

"Jacqueline is special," Grams said simply.

"Grams..." I forced the burning anger down, but didn't let go of it—if I did I'd have to deal with the fear that would stop my breath if I had any. I turned to Dupree. "They filled my coffin with holy water. At least I'm pretty sure they didn't do all that just to give me a bath. It should have been an acid bath to me, but like Grams says, I'm *special*. Holy things don't bother me—please don't spread it around."

Paul ran fingers through his hair. "This is nuts."

"No, really? It's all kinds of insane. *Why?*"

"Be sensible, child. You have enemies." Grams lowered my foot and I tucked it under my robe.

"No Grams, I meant why like this? If Acacia's sire still wanted me, all he'd have had to do was wait for tonight when every vamp in town will be at the Midnight Ball—it's not like he knows I'm leaving town." No, he had come after me in my home, where people I loved...

I forced my fists to unclench, looked at my hands. My nails had left bloody gouges in my palms. I'd let myself come home thinking I could keep Grams *safe*. Had they waited till she had gone, or had it been lucky timing? Even if I left now, if *they* didn't know and she was home next time, could her mojo really protect her? *So make sure everybody knows.*

I raised my head. "I'm going to the party, Grams."

Her lips tightened. "You are leaving tonight, child."

"No." I shook my head. "I'll be safe enough at the Midnight Ball, and afterwards I'll use the safe house one last time—fly out tomorrow night. Casper can put up with company for one more day."

Paul nodded. "So every vamp in town will know you're leaving, *chèr*. That'd work."

"No, child." Grams' voice was steel, but her fingers shook as she closed her first-aid kit. "This is too dangerous, and you do not fool me. You are hoping— You—"

"I will go with her, Mrs. Bouchard," Paul said. "Keep her safe, me. Safer than I did last time."

"And I'll help, Ma'am," Dupree seconded as I rolled my eyes. He and Paul weren't related, but now they looked exactly alike. Paul had told Dupree what the monster had done to his sister, and together they were two bayou boys looking for some justice even if I wasn't sure what dog Paul had in the fight.

How freaking wonderful. Two knights in shining armor. I kept my mouth shut. It would make Grams feel better.

Whether it helped or not—and truthfully I didn't expect even Acacia's sire to be bug-nuts enough to try anything direct at the *Midnight Ball*—Grams didn't push it. Instead she got busy pulling in favors to make sure we were ready; Liz Alary, one of her longtime clients, owned a costume shop (big business in this town). I headed upstairs while she summoned Liz to save the day.

Liz was a huge woman, but sharp and as forceful as an avalanche. My bedroom hadn't been blown up in the excitement although there were bullet holes in interesting places from where Paul and Dupree tried to fight their way into my crypt. Showering and changing and packing a few things for the trip, I came back down to find she'd arrived and trapped my two protectors. She'd obviously embraced our plan and ruthlessly plundered her stock, including some special-ordered pieces, to help us out. *Help* being relative; I wasn't sure either of the boys appreciated it.

I found Paul kitted up as a steampunk werewolf. He wore a long brown duster with plenty of room to hide his police-issue firearm, and he'd added a second shoulder holster to carry one of my Desert Eagles. He wore a very fancy face-covering wolfmask (dyed rabbit fur?) under a bowler hat. Under the duster he wore a collared shirt with suspenders and a gadget belt holding up a pair of side-buckled pants.

Liz had outfitted Dupree in red cardinal's robes, complete with sash and a big golden gear on a chain where a cardinal's pectoral cross would be. The robes gave him plenty of room to hide his weapons of choice, and Liz had completed the costume with a smooth white Mardi Gras halfmask (gilded clockwork monocle sculpted over one eye) and a red wide-brimmed hat to match the robes.

Neither looked happy.

"Don't laugh," Paul growled (yes, growled!), and I did my best. I was *so* getting a picture. But it was my turn.

"Jacqueline, come here." Liz drew me into the parlor. She'd used screens to turn it into a dressing room and she had me out of my fresh clothes faster than I'd have thought possible, then started handing me items. Five minutes later, she had me dressed in goth steampunk. Was that even allowed?

First there were white knickers that were practically silk shorts, then a short white petticoat and sheer white stockings. Then she passed me a long sleeved high collared white shirt and a clipped black skirt. The skirt could be worn long, but the silver clips just below the tight waist raised it to expose the edges of the petticoat. A tight black padded leather vest dispensed with the need for a bra, and a close fitting open jacket with lots of buckles and gear shaped cufflinks and epaulets finished the costume.

A tiny top hat, lace gloves, and matching black

umbrella accessorized the outfit—I could use a pair of my own buckled boots. My lace half-mask didn't disguise me at all, but that was the point; I needed to be seen.

Liz circled around me, pulling edges and talking to herself while I wondered if I was ever going to get away from ruffles and skirts again. I sighed philosophically. The flounces the skirt clips and petticoat created let me hide my Kel-Tec in its thigh holster at the top of my stockings, and the jacket sleeves hid my stakes.

We scattered for last-minute jobs, but before Grams let me out of her sight she pulled me aside and into Legba's room. It was small and close and smelled of snake, but shelves ringed the wall at chest height, filled with pieces of Gram's craft that she wanted to keep safe.

Reaching up, she retrieved a small wood box. Opened, it held a black leather gris-gris pouch on a braided loop of string. She held out the box.

"You will wear this, Jacqueline. You will not open it, or let anyone else touch it, and it will bring help to you."

My throat closed up, but I nodded. Grams waited until I'd opened my collar and tucked it away, and then surprised me with a hug.

"You *will* come home, child," she said.

Chapter Twenty Four

Vampires are the most self-involved creatures imaginable.
They have to be so into the whole creature of darkness
thing that they are willing to give up all natural human
ties. Family? Can't have kids, can't fall in love with
someone and grow old together. But they have style. In
fact, that's pretty much what they're all about.

Jacky Bouchard, *The Artemis Files.*

Lalaurie House glowed, all three floors lit, shutters open to
the night. Big doormen in black kept the street party away
from the front entryway while one of them—Scarhead—
checked the guest list. The Midnight Ball began at
midnight; the death of the day, the darkest hour of the
dark moon, etcetera.

At sundown I'd called the Master of Ceremonies' man
Vessy to RSVP and let him know the faces we'd be wearing
tonight, then we'd sallied forth to join the Dark Moon

Krewe. MC had founded the little Mardi Gras marching society three years ago out of local vamps and their courts, and our foot parade started at St. Louis Cemetery (where else?) to dance through the Quarter to Lalaurie House following a brass band pulled on decked out bicycle cabs. Vessy, dressed like an undertaker who'd been attacked by a neon sign, stood in an open carriage pulled by a couple of vamps in chess piece horse costumes, and tossed silver and white beads—Dark Moon Krewe's signature throws— to the crowds.

Cheerfully lubricated partiers flowed around us, pushing and laughing, half in costume, half enjoying the wild scenery, goth black mixing with Mardi Gras purple and gold. Less than a hundred guests would be allowed into the exclusive rooms of Lalaurie House, but the rest of the krewe and an accretion of fellow dancers were taking over the street. The jazz band played for them as we pushed towards the door, Paul on my right, Dupree on my left.

Paul felt steady, and I knew where he was without looking at him. I couldn't see Dupree's face at all, but the way he'd stripped and cleaned his gun, sitting at Gram's kitchen table, had said enough. He'd counted the blessed silver bullets Father Graff had given him twice. While I scanned the crowd and Paul grumbled under his mask, Dupree... flexed his hands. Honestly, he was starting to make me nervous.

Scarhead greeted us at the door and waved us through with a wink—I'd been prepared to push a little *these aren't the droids you're looking for* influence to avoid a weapons check, but it looked like MC was trusting us.

By modern standards, Lalaurie House was a mini-mansion; one hundred guests plus staff filled it to bursting. The rooms to the right of the entryway had been opened into one large reception room. Two fireplaces occupied one wall, but the street wall held arched floor-to-ceiling windows behind iron grills. A second reception room to the left had been turned into a *small* ballroom. Servers moved soundlessly across the black-and-white checkered floor, through a crowd of masked faces every shade of goth and carnival. Halloween and Mardi Gras had slammed together for this Midnight Ball.

Looking around, I decided Halloween had won. Between the other night and now, MC's decorator had thrown around enough black crepe to make Lalaurie House look like a Victorian home in deep mourning. *Who died? Oh wait, we did.* The masked servers wore black tuxes *and* black armbands as they bore trays of wine for everyone (red wine, what else?) and finger foods for the living. In the small ballroom across the hall, by the light of *real* candles, tapered and white, partners elegantly but carefully wheeled about the floor—to *Midnight Waltz*, of course, sure to be followed by *Flor De Noche*, *Wake*, and just about anything else by Adam Hurst; MC was a huge fan but I could feel my will to live fading.

Both Paul and Dupree moved in tighter and I almost laughed, but we had a problem. The usual Midnight Ball etiquette called for attending vampires to wear a black rose somewhere (really a red rose with black tones), but for tonight's masque all bets were off and I couldn't tell the vamps from the breathers. Anybody could be anybody. I couldn't see Leroy or Sable—or I could be looking right at them—but I recognized Belladonna despite her owl mask; she'd ditched her goth punk leather and wore a backless, armless ballroom gown to display an amazing set of corset piercings. The velvet-laced rows of gold piercings ran from the top of her butt to up between the angel wing tattoos covering her shoulder blades. I'd seen both before at the goth-tats party where I got my *Shit Happens* tramp stamp.

Maybe Liz had known something; nearly every guest I could see wore an animal mask. Fur, leather, feathers: a menagerie, in black, in purple and gold, in every other color, filled Lalaurie House tonight.

So now what? I took a wine glass from a passing server, sipped, then carefully *didn't* spit. The wine was fine, but Darren had just sidled up to me. *What?*

He didn't wear a mask, but he walked hunched over, had three days of beard stubble, serious bed hair (with something dark and sticky pulling strands up above one ear), chalky skin, fake blood on his lips, and a skeletal, demented grin. His clothes looked Victorian-era, complete with detaching collar, suspenders, and turned back cuffs. The white shirt was missing buttons, and the whole outfit looked like he'd crawled through ditches. *What?*

He winked at me, pulled a...cockroach? out of his pocket, and crunched down on it. Chewed wetly, really—it was a licorice bug.

"Who *are* you?" I blurted.

He wiggled his eyebrows, giggled maniacally.
"Renfield, beautiful lady. Who else would serve my dark
master? He promised me beautiful things! Will you go to
him?" He pointed, and I turned to see the Master of
Ceremonies standing by the stairs, Vessy beside him. He
wore a black and white tuxedo under an opera cloak. His
mask was gone, replaced by whiteface makeup, rouged
lips, and arched eyebrows, his hair slicked back into a
widow's peak. He was Arnold Schwarzenegger channeling
Bela Lugosi.

Oh. My. God. I stared from "Renfield" to MC and my
image of him shifted, like the ink portrait of the old
woman who turns into a young lady wearing pearls if you
looked at it differently.

MC *knew*. He knew this place was a Disney mansion
and he was *laughing*.

"Welcome, my dear Mina." He bowed and kissed my
gloved hand when I reached him, causing sighs of envy
among the Victorian ladies orbiting him. Vessy leaned
down to whisper in his boss's ear before gliding away
through the crowd.

He raised an eyebrow at my companions. "May I steal
her from you, gentlemen? I promise to return her to you
safe."

Paul nodded behind his wolf mask, stepping back, and
Dupree had no choice but to follow his lead. Turning and
drawing his cloak aside, MC drew on my hand to lead me
up the stairs. In the upstairs hallway, Scarhead stood by

the door to the library; he must have changed posts as soon as he let us in, and now he opened the door and stood aside. Even here, MC had lit the room with a candelabra over the fireplace.

A wine bottle, opened to breathe, and two glasses sat on a side table. MC poured, handed me a glass with a half-bow and flourish, invited me to sit and followed suit. I rested my folded umbrella on the arm of my chair and he did the same with his cane, sitting back to swirl his wine in the glass and test its bouquet. He ventured a sip, smiled archly.

"I can say all sorts of things about its nose and palate, if you like."

Wound tight as a spring, I looked at Count Dracula and still had to sit on the urge to laugh.

"I thought you didn't drink...wine."

His smile widened. I sipped my own, decided to try.

"Are you Leroy's sire?"

His smile didn't waver. "Why do you ask?"

"Because your pet lawyer lives with him. Because I don't know any more about you than I do about him but I know bullshitting when I see it."

"I do not possess that gift, and have only met one vampire who does. Until you arrived in town, I thought her unique. Is Acacia well? Have you learned who enthralled her and how?" Above the smile his eyes were steady, watchful.

Looking at MC, I made a second decision. "She will be. As soon as the DSA is done *debriefing* her I'm going to find her and make sure she forgets everything as far back as the night she met me."

Now the smile froze.

"You work for the government?" His voice didn't change, but his eyes were ice.

Did. They cut me loose. For the first time since I'd met him, MC looked like what he was: a predator. I hugged my wineglass to my breasts, feeling the pressure of the gris-gris pouch beneath my shirt, and switched hands to sip my wine while letting my free hand fall to rest beside my thigh, ready to draw and start shooting. I smiled back.

"Did you think I was here just to chase vamps who like young blood? The cops can do that."

Neither of us looked away, neither of us extended so much as a wisp of influence.

"I'm flying back to Chicago tomorrow night," I said.

"May I ask why?"

I told him about a monster and serial killer, a vampire using V-Juice to create his own little army. He deserved that much.

"Are you running?" he asked when I finished. His eyes had warmed and he didn't look *dangerous* anymore. He didn't sound angry, or disappointed. Mildly curious. I put down my glass.

"Yes. The feds will get him now. Everyone leaves a trail somewhere and now that they know how he works they'll find him. Until then I'm dangerous to be around."

He didn't ask; he had to know about today. And he was quick.

"So you're here tonight to announce your departure. And what of the favor you wanted of me?"

I'll get it another way. I shrugged, setting down my glass, and smiled. "Would you look at the time?"

"The clock is behind you." But he stood smoothly, collecting his cane. "One dance, my dear. And I will make the announcement for you. Regretfully, of course."

We didn't make it to the door.

The explosion threw the door, in two pieces and a cloud of slivers, across the room. One piece clipped MC, throwing him back over his chair and barely missing the candelabra. The other spun past as I rose, only to be flattened by Scarface's body—tossed like a rag doll after the door. My Kel-Tec skittered across the hardwood floor.

"Get them!" someone screamed, certainly the stupidest, most obvious command possible in the circumstances. I promised to suggest alternatives when I caught him, and went to mist—to get hammered back into flesh as *three* vamps dropped on me. I shrieked as one drove a spike through my right hand, nailing me to the floor with the strength of the damned. I grabbed my spiker's ear and ripped it away before his buddy got the second spike through my shoulder.

Then they were off me as I clawed uselessly at my shoulder, breath a thin wail. Meaty thunks behind me attested to MC's fight, but it ended quick. A roar shook the room, rage and frustration, a familiar cleaver-on-flesh sound, and his head bounced across my angle of vision. Distantly, through the rage and pain, screams echoed up from downstairs. Screams of fear, of crowd panic; I knew that one.

I turned my head, ignoring the pain fogging my brain, and stared at a pair of buckled shoes and white knee-socks. Sable smiled down at me, quite pleased.

"Darling Jacqueline," he said. "It appears you've missed your flight."

Chapter Twenty Five

Werewolves are closer to nature. It sticks in their teeth.

Jacky Bouchard, *The Artemis Files.*

My grave in New Orleans was going to read *Here lies Jaqueline Bouchard: too dumb to live.* It would be empty of course, since I would be ash.

The attack today really had been a Last Shot before I left town, it *had* to be—after five years I knew something about hunting somebody, and *anything* else would have been easier to set up.

But if Emerson hadn't known I was leaving, his department didn't know so the leak couldn't have come from there. *Gray* had known, but if the DSA field office had a leak...no, they were too small and paranoid for that. Which left only one other person who had known my plans, because I'd *told* him last night.

How could I have possibly missed it? All seven known

victims—the two poor tortured girls, the five drug victims, Acacia—were blondes. Whose favorites were always *Lucys*?

"And what are you thinking, darling girl?" Sable asked, tapping my spiked shoulder with his cane. I hissed, took a breath.

"That you won't find Stephanie. You are such an asshat."

He frowned and dug into my shoulder.

"Master?" One of his hoodsmen stepped in from the hall, red machete in hand. "We've got the downstairs." Below the hood he was wearing a server's outfit. *Duh. Come in as the caterers...* Sable and three in here, only two downstairs? They must have enthralled more live minions.

Sable nodded. "Excellent work. Adrian, Gregor, see that everyone is gathered in the receiving room. I need to chat with everyone."

I giggled. "Everyone's name is smarter than yours. Did you let them pick their own?" He leaned on his cane and I screamed. His merry little group snickered.

"Why no, I did not. Belladonna had that privilege. But then, I named her and her sister." So I'd been wrong about Bell, too.

I managed to stop screaming, pulled in another breath. "So. What. Now?"

"Now? Now I decide who dies." He waved his hand. "They'll just...disappear. Nobody has seen *my* face tonight, and nobody will know who has killed our silly Master of Ceremonies. But every vampire that I allow to live will know they have a new *master*." He withdrew his cane, swung it to lightly tap my cheek. "A few will resist, of course. My minions will hunt them down in their crypts, make them examples. It will be very tedious, but I'll have you to entertain me."

I stared up at him. He honestly had no *idea*. He thought he could *win*. I had no breath to laugh.

He took my silence for surrender and his smile grew, his eyes sparkled merrily. "Diego, Leonid, let's rearrange our darling girl. She looks uncomfortable." I kicked uselessly as his remaining hoodsmen joined him in leaning over me. They knelt on my legs.

Sable set his cane on a chair and untied his cravat. "If it helps, you may close your eyes and think of England."

And Paul ripped his head off.

I felt like Carrie at the prom. You know—when her fun-loving classmates dump pigs' blood on her? Sable had been busy—I could taste just about every blood type but O-negative—and at two hundred plus pounds, minus a few for the head, he didn't feel good landing on my shoulder either. I hissed through my teeth when big wolfy Paul threw him off me, screamed again when he wrapped his plate-sized claws around my hand and shoulder and pulled me up from the floor.

I kept screaming, slammed my open hand with its iron spike into number two hoodsman's head. He staggered and the second one unfroze. Paul casually grabbed his head and used him to beat his buddy. Neither tried to mist as Paul turned them into hamburger.

Pulling out the spike, I found a machete and finished them. They'd thank me someday; I was pretty sure Paul was considering digestion just to make them stay down.

The library looked like a mad artist had expressed himself all over the walls. And the shelves. And the furniture. I pushed a bloody tangle of hair out of my eyes, turned my shoulder to Paul. "Would you mind?" He huffed, got a grip on my shoulder, carefully pinched the spike between thumb and index finger, and yanked it out. I couldn't keep the scream down—it had gone through *bone*.

He threw it into the fireplace, where it clattered on the tiles. Then he changed.

"Well that was disappointing," I said. I hadn't caught it the first time, and it wasn't like in the movies. One moment he was a foot taller and *really* hairy, the next his huge *wolfness* faded like an afterimage, like a mirage that had been painted in by CGI or not-so-solid spirit. No screaming, no warping of flesh and bone, no ick. At least his clothes were properly shredded, except for the duster and his spandex werewolf pants.

"I could always groan a little and stagger around, *chèr*. Are you good?"

"Do I *look* like I'm good?" I pulled at my bloody jacket. "Liz is going to kill both of us." The hole in my hand had closed before I put the machete down.

"You *grandmère* isn't going to be too happy either."

"How did you—"

"I followed the guy dressed as Baron Samedi out and

up the backstairs. He said you'd need help. Showed me the back way in, then he wasn't there." *And don't ask*, his eyes said. "So now what?"

I'd like to know too. Okay, at least three, maybe four of Sable's faithful progeny downstairs with the guests. Plus minions, Belladonna? Two of us, plus Dupree, who—not being insane—was probably waiting sensibly with the crowd for the situation to develop. Leroy? Other vamps might join in, but becoming a creature of the night didn't make someone a fighter; if they were on our side, how useful could they be?

I tried my cellphone. No connection; if they were at all clever, they'd set up a jammer to swamp the tower signal.

We could get out, call reinforcements—but even if they expected their master to take his time with me, eventually somebody was going to come upstairs to see what was taking so long. Then...anybody's guess. I wanted to try and put MC back together, even the odds a little, but the night I'd been chopped Leroy had spirited me away to a safe place before doing it. Which meant it probably took a little while, and we couldn't wait for him any more than we could wait for the cops. *This bites.*

I collected my Desert Eagle and shoulder holster from Paul, found and holstered my Kel-Tec, hefted my machete, gave Sable a good kick. It was time for them to meet Artemis.

"They're waiting for their fearless leader to come down and talk to them. Let's go talk."

It felt way too familiar: unknown number of bad guys,

lots of fragile civilians, no time to bring overwhelming force and squash them like bugs. But my blood rose anyway as I moved down the hallway, listened at the stairs.

Behind me, Paul went back to fur. Downstairs somebody was crying, scared, but not desperate or in pain. I looked back at Paul, pointed left with the machete; they'd have collected everyone in one place, and all their attention would be on their "guests." When Paul nodded, I turned and walked down the stairs, boots silent on the carpeted steps.

One, two, three, four, five, not-so-silent steps on the tiled floor of the entry hall, slow and not at all alarming like running steps would have been. One hoodsman, one armed minion in the doorway, both starting to turn. Step-step-*swing*.

Hoodsman's head came off. Paul took the minion's gun away by grabbing his gun hand and swinging him into the wall. The screaming started as I went to mist. Paul howled loud enough to shake the paintings on the walls as I swept up to get a ceiling view.

Yes! Dupree ripped his mask off, pulled his .45 full of Church-blessed bullets from beneath his robes, and started banging away while screaming at everyone to *Get Down!* The hoodsman closest to him practically exploded. An unmasked Leroy sliced into another with his saber—he'd come as a pirate, go figure—moving like he was dancing. Most costumed vamps rose to mist and fled, but not all of them; fastidious Vessy and a white swan turned on the last hoodsman. I went to flesh, landed on another minion and swung. His gun and hand sprang away in a fan of blood. Turning to look for a target, I nearly died again. Belladonna's machete bit, a passing kiss beneath my ear as I fell back into mist.

"Shit!" she screamed, and followed.

Through the screaming, the shooting, the chaos as civilians tried to flee, we danced in and out of mist, *pushing*, racing each other to flesh, leaping off again. Mist-flesh-*swing*-mist-repeat, *YES!* Sliced her arm, blood running. Dropping her blade, she leaped, grabbed my arm and pulled me *into* mist. *What?* Back down, she controlled our landing; my face smacked the tile floor and I lost my borrowed machete.

Then the fire started.

Crepe *burns*.

The fire raced around the walls, from wreaths of "black roses" to black-draped portraits as exploding panic knocked over more freestanding candelabras. Somebody's stray rounds hit the bar and the spilled hard liquor and decorations went up like a torch. Belladonna laughed in my face, giggling madly as the room filled with smoke.

I could hear Dupree shouting, one turn in our dance and I saw him standing by an open window, grillwork unlatched, throwing guests out into the street.

I *liked* that boy.

"Sable's dead!" I shouted, trying to shake Belladonna. She laughed again and twisted us to the floor, way stronger than me. How much blood did she have in her?

"He was an idiot! I was going to kill him myself!"

I ducked clawing nails as she went for my eyes. Mist-flesh-mist-flesh, and she wrapped her legs around my waist, screaming in my face. Mist-flesh, she controlled the angle and we bounced off fleeing guests, smacked a burning wall, fell. Mist-flesh-mist-flesh, and my backbone ground loudly as she laughed. If she broke my back, did it count as decapitation?

She pushed my face away and leaned in, binding legs leaving only my right arm free.

"My plan," she whispered. "His place. I let him have his toys, and nobody will look for me after tonight." And she bit me.

"No!" I gasped as liquid pleasure exploded from my neck, flooded my brain. I started to sink. *No no no no nononono*— My flailing hand caught, and I ripped the corset piercings out of her back, popping like a burst zipper all the way down.

She *screamed*, my stolen blood spattered my face as she arched reflexively away from the agony, and I brought up a knee to break her hold. Mist-flesh, and I held a needle sharp stake in my hand. Mist-flesh and the stake bit into her naked, bloodied back just below the lowest feather of her angel wing tattoo. Her scream rose to a shriek, cut as we hit the floor and my weight drove the stake deeper. She lay still.

I spit, slid off her, took a breath past the half-closed slice in my neck and looked up at the smoke filled air.

Anyone who could get had got; I shared the reception

room with shortened vamps, groaning and silent bodies, and a furry and singed Paul. This time I managed to stand before he could help me up.

He looked down at Belladonna. Growled.

"*No*," I said, sighed. "Time to clean up."

Chapter Twenty Six

We defy augury; there's a special providence in the fall of a sparrow. If it be now, 'tis not to come; if it be not to come, it will be now; if it be not now, yet it will come: the readiness is all.

William Shakespeare, *Hamlet.*

Look. Stuff happens. You do what you do, or you don't.

Jacky Bouchard, *The Artemis Files.*

"You did threaten to burn it to the ground," MC said. From what I could see of his face in the flashing lights, he didn't seem too bothered.

Paul had pulled vamp heads and bodies and Belladonna's staked corpse out of the ground floor. As the one who didn't need to breathe, I'd gone back upstairs. I'd wrapped MC in the library curtains before tossing him out the window and over the balcony, which was more than I did for the two hoodsmen. *They* would be picking gravel out of their teeth when they rose in Emerson's lockup.

I'd left Sable—in fact I'd smashed MC's liquor cabinet and poured on the hard stuff to help him burn. I wanted to feel bad about that. *Maybe later.*

I shrugged. "Urban renewal. And it's not 'to the ground.' " The roof fell in, throwing up a great plume of sparks while firemen yelled. I winced. "Not yet."

Being busy, I'd used the curtains to keep his head attached to his neck while I did other things, and by my watch it had taken close to two hours for him to rise. "Other things" included calling Gray to suggest he beat feet over to Sable's before Emerson's boys did; the DSA would turn a drug-assisted master vampire into a wannabe trying to take over the vampire scene. *Move along, nothing to see here...* I told him to tell his bosses I was coming for Acacia.

After I took care of a few things.

I glanced at MC. *Count Dracula* looked more like Renfield now. Darren had gotten out fine; in fact none of the guests had been killed in the fight or the fire. Bullet holes, trampling injuries, smoke inhalation, oh yeah. But no fatalities, a major miracle that had me rethinking who saints listened to. Or Baron Samedi.

He caught me looking. "Yes?"

"It's your turn."

A deep laugh. "I suppose it is. I could argue that you didn't *deliver* Sable to me, but such tactics are for lawyers. Come. It is not far."

Fire hoses ran everywhere, misted spray wet the streets while fire and water ate everything MC owned, and only two hours remained of the night, but he turned and walked away. Technically we weren't free to go. We were witnesses, suspects, whatever (Emerson had been *sarcastic*), but a blanket of influence pushed us past the police at the perimeter. I didn't look for Paul or Dupree. Paul was with Emerson doing cop things (actually trying to find the Baron Samedi nobody else had seen, and I wished him luck with that), and Dupree had gone to the hospital to get a bullet out of his thigh.

MC proceeded down Royal Street and turned south. It didn't take me long to guess where we were going. Darren opened the street door to the *Salle D'Armes*. He'd cleaned up, and he waved us in with his usual cheerful smile. Leroy stood behind him.

"Jacob," Leroy said, nodding to MC.

"Marc." MC nodded back.

"Jacqueline."

"Really? Do we all know our names now?"

Darren laughed, and I saw a hint of a twist in Leroy's mouth as he stepped aside.

"Darren? Could you get Jacob something to drink? I'll show Jacqueline downstairs." They went one way while we went another. I shouldn't have been surprised when Leroy led me back to the kitchen I'd woken up in and down to the "guestroom" he'd given me the first time.

He pushed the metal door open with a squeal of heavy hinges, and when he flipped on the light I could see he'd been down here earlier. The bolts holding the steel chest to the concrete floor had been removed.

"Lift your end," he instructed, taking hold of the other. Together we lifted the chest out of its brackets and set it to the side. It had to weigh at least a ton—five husky living weightlifters probably couldn't have moved it.

Beneath was a locked panel, which he opened. Beneath that was Sleeping Beauty.

"Her name," said Leroy, "is Claire. We grew up together in La Tuque—in Quebec."

No freaking way.

My legs gave out and I sat without thought, leaning closer and blinking as if it would change what I saw. She was a Mina, all dark curls around a pale narrow face. Laid out in a long black gown, hands clasped loosely beneath her breasts, she looked like a wax-museum display of the fairy tale; perfect, but too pale and fragile to be pretty.

Leroy knelt and tucked a fugitive lock behind her ear.

"She was always sick, an underdeveloped heart that made her unwell. I would bring her schoolwork when she couldn't attend, but when she was thirteen her family moved to Montreal so that she could be near specialists. We continued to call and write, and I'd visit."

He looked up. "For Claire, life was a fight with her heart, with her blood. Along with everything else, she was anemic. Her medication—" he laughed "—her medication made her skin sensitive to sunlight. Can you wonder why she fell in love with vampires? Romances, thrillers, any vampire story. Every time illness would keep her in her bed, which was more and more often, she'd read a hundred more. She died at twenty-five."

"And rose?"

"And rose. A breakthrough, of course."

"But—people dying of illnesses *don't*. Have breakthroughs, I mean." Shockingly, Leroy chuckled.

"How fortunate, then, that a thief shot her. Wouldn't you agree? Through the heart, proving God has a sense of humor. A black one."

I couldn't disagree there. "So what happened?"

"Claire could hardly hide what had happened, and didn't want to. She became quite the celebrity. By then I was living in Toronto, training for the Olympics, and she came to visit. I took her clubbing. She'd never been able to go. Three men attacked us—hunters, I found out. She killed one, the others ran, but not before they killed me."

I closed my eyes. I could imagine how an Olympian in training, a champion fencer, had died. It wouldn't have been standing behind her. "You bled out."

"In her arms. But not before she gave some of her own blood to me. She believed the stories, and it was all she could think to do."

Crap. I looked down at the sleeping master vamp. "So you took her and you ran."

"She is not a fighter, my Claire. Her story was very public, but I could disappear. She could not hide, even here, but, you know that if we do not drink, we sleep?" I nodded, throat tight. "So she sleeps, and I keep her safe. And what will you do?"

I didn't go to the safe house; one call and Gray had a driver pick me up to swing me by Grams so I could change and grab my bag. He delivered me to a private airport as the sky shaded to blue. The armed loadmaster promised me that they would fly me hangar-to-hangar without ever seeing sunlight, and I believed him; I was still useful to them, even if Emerson had sworn not to let me near a police operation again. Gray's bosses had agreed—I had an appointment at Camp Necessity to take away Acacia's nightmare.

Then I could go *home*. Hope would be happy to see me, Gray would be happy *not* to see me while he cleaned up, and I could forget about an innocently sleeping seed of Vampire Armageddon.

Every window in the small passenger section had been shut and taped over, but I felt the sunrise as the wheels left the runway. I didn't fight it. They'd provided a thick shipping box and I took one of the seat pillows in with me. Closing the lid, I released my breath and slept the sleep of the dead.

The End.

ABOUT THE AUTHOR

Marion G. Harmon is a lifelong bibliophile who, after twenty years of asking questions like "What would superheroes be like in the real world?" and "Really, what is the upside to being a blood-sucking fiend of the night?", decided to write about it. The answers are sometimes weird, and after failing to find a publisher, he decided to self-publish so he could stop rewriting the same stories. To his surprise, a lot of people like his books.

He lives in Las Vegas, where he will continue to write as long as readers keep paying to hear about Astra and Artemis and other characters he gives page-space to.

CPSIA information can be obtained at www.ICGtesting.com
Printed in the USA
LVOW10s0934091114

412747LV00012B/529/P